Echoes in the Static

Love, Loss and the Power of the Unseen

Copyright

Author: Tony Warner
Title: Echoes in the Static
© 2024, Tony Warner
Self-published
(Contact: psiwarbook@gmail.com)

All rights reserved.
No part of this publication may be reproduced, stored in a retrieval system, stored in a database and / or published in any form or by any means, electronic, mechanical, photocopying, recording or otherwise, without the prior written permission of the author.

Acknowledgments

To all my dedicated readers: thank you for choosing to spend your valuable time with these stories. Your support is everything.

For those of you whose names appear in these stories with or without their knowledge, I offer my deepest thanks. You have made each story come alive.

And as always, my thanks go to my family for their support and encouragement.

Tony

The Gate

I survey the Gate with a mixture of satisfaction, elation, and awe. It worked! It really worked! Finally, I have something to show for all my work. It's taken two years of research, long days of study and countless sleepless nights, followed by five months of designing, fabricating and building, plus two more months of unsuccessful trials.

And now, here it was, a black, two metre disc hanging in the air before me. I tried in vain to contain a huge grin that spread across my face. At last! My theories and calculations were correct. I was right all along. The multiverse exists. The black disc in front of me proves it.

I remember to breathe and draw in a deep breath, letting it out slowly.

Pulling myself together, I examine the readouts and the text slowly scrolling on the screen in front of me. All normal. Great. Absolutely fantastic. It's stable, just as I predicted.

I stand from my chair, approach the disc and peer around it. My theories predicted that it would have no width. Sure enough, when I look at it edge on, there's nothing there. But as I move further, it reappears exactly as it should.

I'm more than happy. I'm ecstatic.

"Bring the drone," I instruct one of the lab staff.

Sam picks up a case from beside his console and walks up to the disc. He sets it down, opens it, and removes a small drone. He takes a few minutes to power it up. While he does so, I walk back to my command station and resume my seat.

"Make sure you're recording," I tell him needlessly.

Behind me, two more of my staff, Daisy and Shafiq, are monitoring the disc carefully.

"No radiation, no heat signature and no magnetic anomalies," Daisy calls out.

Just as my calculations predicted, I think to myself.

"Drone is ready," Sam announces as he stands, brushing a lock of mousey brown hair from his forehead. He's one of my most trusted colleagues. Without him, I doubt I would be here today. His engineering skills complimented my theories perfectly. His ability to build anything I could think up was nothing short of amazing.

"Send it through," I instruct him. "Shafiq, route the video to my console."

The screen in front of me flickers as Shafiq complies, and the video feed from the drone appears. I watch with bated breath as it slowly moves towards the black disc. Daisy and Sahfiq join me, standing close behind as the drone passes through the blackness of the disc.

Daisy draws in a sharp intake of breath as the drone transmits the first image of a parallel world. A world beyond the Gate. A world that exists next to this one.

I frown. The image is not what I expect to see. My calculations and the control settings of the Gate show that the world we are viewing should be very similar to our own. It's not.

"What's that?" asks Shafiq.

It's a building. But no ordinary building. It's huge, black and ominous, stretching high into the sky. But it's the sky that shocks me. It's not blue or grey and overcast like it is here. Instead, it's purple, orange and green. The vast building is some distance away, a tower of obsidian, standing alone in a plain of orange sand. This is not the world I expected at all.

Have I made a mistake in my calculations?

The four of us are speechless as we view the alien world. Sam on his controller, the rest of us at my console. I'm trying to make sense of it, trying to figure out what we were seeing, when Sam gives a yelp.

I refocus my attention on the screen. Something moves. I can't make it out. It's moving fast, very fast. All I see is a blurred outline. Then suddenly there is a crash as something passes through the Gate and crashes into Sam, knocking him over. He loses his grip on the drone controller, which slides across the room to thump against a wall.

"CLOSE IT!" a female voice screams. "CLOSE IT NOW!"

I stand quickly. My chair flies back, catching Shafiq in the shins. Beyond my console, in front of the Gate, a woman lies on the floor, her limbs tangled with Sam's. She's aiming a pistol-like weapon at the Gate.

Shafiq grunts in pain and dances backwards, cursing.

"Holy shit!" exclaims Daisy.

"Get off!" Sam shouts from the floor.

Seconds pass as we all try to make sense of what's happening.

"CLOSE IT!" the woman screams again.

I open my mouth to ask why, to ask what's going on, when she tips her head back and looks up at me with wild eyes.

I instantly recognise those eyes. I see them in the mirror every morning. They're mine!

Seconds pass as we stare at each other, then she screams again.

"SHUT THE GATE. SHUT IT NOW!"

I'm shocked and frozen. I don't know what to do. Why is she so insistent that the Gate is closed? More importantly, why does she look like me? She has the same blonde hair, the same blue eyes, the same dimples in her cheeks. She's wearing some sort of leather outfit, maybe for protection? The trousers are brown and straight cut; her top, some kind of thick black vest with straps. Bullet proof? Fashion? She's dirty, there's dried blood on her chin and the hands gripping the pistol-like weapon are grubby and caked with grime. A leather cord holds back her matted and tangled hair.

"BECKY!" she screams at me.

My eyes go wide. She knows my name.

"BECKY! SHUT THE GATE!"

With an effort, I flick my gaze away from the woman on the floor to the Gate and gasp in astonishment.

A grey green tentacle as thick as my waist is protruding through the Gate and is feeling its way along the floor towards Sam and the stranger.

My mouth falls open. What's happening? What is this thing? Is it a snake?

"BECKY!" she screams my name again.

This time, I push my shock aside. I smash the heel of my hand down hard on the large red button on my console.

The Gate closes instantly severing the sickly coloured tentacle. It writhes and flops around on the floor. It must be six or seven feet long and thick. Thicker than a snake, well, no snake I've ever seen. It crashes and coils around the laboratory, knocking over chairs and sweeping cables aside. The severed end leaks fluid that must be blood, but it's like no blood I've ever seen. It's black like tar, but unlike tar, it's much thinner and more like water. It's like sea water that's foaming in a storm. The black foam flies through the air, splashing on the ceiling, the floor, and the equipment. Where it lands, it sizzles and bubbles.

On the floor, the stranger struggles to her feet. She pushes Sam to one side and rolls away from him, leaving him grunting in pain as his head hits a chair leg.

Daisy is muttering to herself, her eyes wide and wild as they dart around the room as if trying to take it all in but can't.

"Shit, shit, shit, shit!" she says over and over.

Behind me, I hear Shafiq breathing heavily. It sounds like he's hyperventilating.

Through all this, I stand dumbfounded, unable to speak. The shock, surprise and sheer astonishment has paralysed me. I can't think as I try to comprehend the scene in front of me.

Then the stranger fires her weapon. Blue fire envelopes the writhing tentacle thing, which is reduced to smoking ash.

Silence blankets the laboratory.

The stranger stands and holsters her weapon. She turns to face me. It's like looking in the mirror. She's me. How can that be possible? It can't be.

Finally, at last, my mind clicks into gear and starts to work. I figure it out. She opens her mouth to speak, but I interrupt her.

"You're me from an alternate reality." It's a statement that I present as a fact, even though I have little evidence apart from the fact that she looks just like me.

She talks immediately after me, continuing my statement as though the same person spoke it. Her voice is identical to mine. The same pitch and the same timbre.

"And you shouldn't have opened a Gate!"

We stare at each other.

Sam gets to his feet, rubbing his forehead and surveying the chaos in the room.

"What the fuck!" he exclaims. "What just happened?"

Daisy and I suppose Shafiq stare incredulously at the stranger.

I approach her slowly, and she follows suit until we are mere inches apart. Slowly, we both raise our right hands in exact mirror fashion to cup each other's cheek. Her cheek is warm, a little slick with sweat, but it feels familiar, as though I am cupping my own. I stare into hazel eyes that are exactly like mine.

"Becky?" asks Daisy. "What's going on? Who is this woman?"

"She came through the Gate! How can she come through the Gate?" Shafiq mumbles behind me.

"She looks just like you!" exclaims Sam.

I can't take my eyes off her.

"That's because she's me," I answer.

She completes my sentence, staring at me.

"From a different world."

"What?" asks Sam. "That's not possible!"

There's a pull, almost like a magnetic force, between this alternate version of me and I. Our faces inch closer until our noses touch. I can feel her warm breath mingling with mine, as well as the warm scent of her sweat and body odour. It doesn't repulse me; instead, it's instantly recognisable and comforting.

"Becky, what's going on?" shouts Daisy.

"Becky?" asks Sam.

Shafiq stumbles forward into my peripheral vision. His eyes are wide in fright, as though he's seen a ghost. His mouth is open, his hands shaking.

I can't help myself, nor can the alternate Becky, we kiss. A spark of electricity thrums in my very core and I jerk back, as does she.

"Jesus!" I hear Sam mutter.

With a tremendous effort of will, I step back, my hand dropping from her cheek. Still staring into each other's eyes, I draw in a tremulous breath and let it out slowly. I can see that she's as deeply affected as I am. In a quavering voice, I manage to speak.

"Daisy, Shafiq, Sam. This is Becky. She's an alternate version of me from a parallel world."

She smiles and I smile back.

Daisy gives a little squeak of noise.

"Fuck off!" snorts Shafiq.

The alternate Becky shifts her eyes from mine to Shafiq.

"Asabhy mat bano," she says to him.

If possible, his eyes go wider.

"Sorry," he mumbles.

"Becky, what are you doing?" asks Daisy. "Why did you kiss her?"

I can tell that she's not happy. The tone in her voice betrays her disgust.

Sam has evidently recovered.

"I didn't mind it," he says in a low, lecherous voice.

The alternate me turns and surveys the room.

"This is your team?" she scoffs in a mocking tone. "I've seen more capable people in a Forin!"

A what?

"What did you think you were doing, opening a Gate like that? Anything could have come through! You were fortunate that it was only a Kiskon! It could have been much worse!"

A Kiskon?

She strides past me to my console and studies the controls intently.

"Primitive," she mutters to herself. "It's a wonder it worked at all!"

Daisy sidles up to me and takes my arm.

"How can she be you?" she hisses. "You said that there wouldn't be any people on the other side of the Gate. How come she's here? And why did you kiss her?"

I watch the alternate Becky as she walks to another console.

"I was wrong," I whisper back. "The world on the other side of the Gate must be very similar to our own. It probably contains copies of each of us. Although." I pause and tilt my head to one side as I piece things together. "It can't be too similar because of that tentacle. But this version of me clearly understands Gate tech." I stop again, then continue. "I'm not sure that two versions of me in one reality are a good idea. There could be repercussions. In fact, there must be!"

My hand goes to my lips as I recall the electric shock I'd felt when we kissed, and my eyes go wide.

"Oh, shit!" I breathe as understanding hits me like a hammer blow.

The idea of duplicates existing in the same reality was unfathomable. It shouldn't be possible, yet it was happening right now in front of me. There were bound to be countless unforeseen issues, like matter and anti-matter colliding and causing a catastrophic release of energy. But that couldn't be the case here. We had just shared a kiss, but what about other interactions? Would our very presence alter history and change the course of the future? Could duplicates even coexist harmoniously in the same world? These questions swirl in my mind, filling me with both uncertainty and dread.

"Yes, exactly, oh shit. Why did you kiss her? What were you thinking?" Daisy hisses at me.

I'm at a loss for words. I have no explanation for my behaviour. It's completely out of character for me. Typically, I'm reserved and introspective. So why did I act that way? Why did I kiss her? I've never kissed anyone in public before. I contemplate this fact, attempting to understand what happened. But I can't. I don't understand why I am drawn to her, and why I still feel that attraction. However, one thing is clear: I enjoyed it.

Sam walks up to stand with the two of us. All three of us watch my duplicate as she prowls around the lab, examining the equipment, occasionally shaking her head and mumbling to herself.

"What's she doing?" he asks. "This is your lab, not hers. She's acting as though she owns the place!" I can hear the annoyance in his voice.

Shafiq joins us.

"What the hell was that snake thing?" he asks. "And who is this woman who looks like you? How come she can speak Hindi?"

I give an exasperated snort.

"I told you, she's me from the world on the other side of the Gate."

"How's that possible?" he asks. "You said that the Gate would connect to a world that was a long way from ours to avoid complications like this. You said that there was no chance of it opening into a world where there would be duplicates of us. You said that could be dangerous!"

I sigh. He's right. I said all those things and I stand by them. The Gate should have connected to a similar world to ours, but not as different as the one I saw in the pictures from the drone, and it definitely shouldn't have been a world where my duplicate lived. What's happened here makes no sense to me.

She seems to be done with her examination of the lab equipment. She stands straight and tall, turning back to face us.

"So, you three idiots been playing with tech you don't understand and opened a Gate to my world. What did you think would happen?"

Once again, I am at a loss for words. She's annoyed and critical of something I've been working on all my life, scolding me as though I were a child. How dare she speak to me like this? I feel my face flush and my limbs shaking uncontrollably as anger rises within me.

"Who the hell are you to criticise us and my lab? You don't know how hard we've been working on this project. Just because you're another version of me, it doesn't give you the right to burst in here and question our motives and work!"

I'm breathless, hot and trembling. I hate losing control like this, but the situation has pushed me over the edge. Part of me wants to lash out, to let all my emotions run wild, but another part of me knows that's not who I am. I desperately try to regain my composure. But before I can, my duplicate speaks up again.

"You realise that you and me being in the same universe could cause any number of repercussions?" She's ignoring my outburst. "You need to send me back now."

She speaks with a sense of authority, her voice calm and collected as if she is accustomed to being in charge and giving orders.

I agree with her. She might be a version of me, and I might have kissed her, but I don't like her. She's critical and annoying. I'm not like that. Am I?

"Yes!" Daisy whispers in my ear. "Let's get rid of her. I don't like her!"

"I agree," Sam whispers in my other ear. "She's a bitch! Send her back!"

"Shaf, check the equipment," I direct him while locking eyes with my duplicate. "Get ready to power-up the Gate."
Shafiq leaps into action, striding to the nearest console. He flicks switches and starts checking displays.

"Sam, check the Gate power lines, Daisy, reset the mainframe."

As my staff hurry to comply with my commands, I walk towards my duplicate once more, my eyes never leaving hers. She waits calmly as I approach, a slight smile on her lips.

"Power up the Gate and I'll go back," she says calmly to me. "Don't open it again, no matter what, it's too dangerous. I know you'll want to, but don't. Trust me."

I feel the magnetism between us once more. It's undeniable and irresistible. Before I know it, we're holding hands and she's pulling me in close.

"I'm sorry," she whispers, her breath mixing with mine as our noses touch.

I'm puzzled and frown.

"What for?" I ask.

She ignores my question and smiles broadly, showing off her white, even teeth.

"Everything is nominal," shouts Shafiq. "Ready when you are."

"Sam? Daisy?" I call out, still staring at my doppelgänger.

"All good," answers Sam.

"Mainframe ready," calls out Daisy.

The alien Becky gazes at me with sorrowful eyes. She pulls me towards her until our bodies press together, and we share another kiss. A thrum of electricity spreads through my body for a longer duration this time, as she prolongs the kiss. Just like before, her lips are velvety and warm, and her breath is sweet and strikingly familiar.

"Gate established," I hear Shafiq, as though from far away, as I fight the wave of hot desire that floods my veins. I know she feels the same way. I can see it in her dilated pupils and her flushed cheeks.

Slowly, and with great effort, we both pull away from each other. I breathe out a deep breath and hear her do the same. She turns to face the black disc that is the Gate and I follow her gaze. Together, hand in hand, we walk towards it.

"Would you like to see?" she asks a little breathlessly.

I know instantly what she means. She's asking me if I would like to see her world. I recall the drone images. The strangely coloured sky and the impossibly tall black building. Curiosity builds within me. I would definitely like to see her world.

"I would," I nod.

She nods back and we step up to the inky black disc. Without hesitation, she acts. She steps through and pulls me after her.

As I step through the Gate, a wall of sweltering heat hits me like a physical force. The bright light of the sun blazes down on me, forcing me to squint and shield my eyes with my hand. Through barely open lids, I take in the scene before me: an endless expanse of orange sand stretching towards the distant horizon. The sand glitters as though it's peppered with tiny golden granules. On my right, I spy the massive black tower rising from the ground. Its sheer size and imposing presence takes my breath away. The base is so wide, I can't even fathom its circumference, and its height seems to touch the sky itself. It's made of an obsidian black material and gives off an intimidating aura that leaves me gaping in awe.

"That's Uramur," says Becky from behind me.

"It's amazing!" I whisper.

"Not really," she answers. "I wouldn't go there if I were you."

I look back at her. She's standing next to the Gate, a sad smile on her face and her weapon in her hand levelled at me.

"What?" I ask.

She gives me a pitying look.

"I've waited and worked for this moment for six months. I'm you, Becky. But I'm not the same as you. I'm a Hopper."

I don't understand.

"What are you talking about?" I ask, perplexed.
She sighs.

"A Hopper is someone who hops between worlds," she explains. "This is my twenty-fourth world. Yours will make it twenty-five."

"Why?" I ask. "Why would you do that?"

"Why not?" she smiles at me. "It's fun. I get to experience the lives of my other selves and their worlds. I'm looking forward to exploring yours."

Dread suddenly fills me. I understand what she's saying. Fuck! She's going to leave me here!

"No," I whisper.

She nods slowly.

"I built a Gate Attractor," she flicks her eyes to her left. I follow her gaze and see a small black box on the ground next to the Gate, a green light shining through vents in its side.

"That's why your Gate opened in this world."

She points her hand weapon at the box and destroys it with blue fire, reducing it to a fused lump.

"Can't have you following me." She says as she swings the weapon back to me.

My skin prickles with the heat, and yet a cold sensation creeps down my back like icy fingers. My breath catches in my throat as I realise her cunning plan. Raw fear washes over me, numbing my thoughts as I struggle to think. She's tricked me and there's nothing I can do.

"I'm going to step back into your world now. You'll be staying here. You're just like me - resourceful, intelligent and capable. Eventually, you'll figure out a way to leave here, but you'll never catch me. I'd forget that idea if I were you."

She pauses.

"For what it's worth, I'm sorry to have to do this to you, but as you know, we can't both live in the same world. It's you or me and I pick me."

I remain rooted to the ground as she slowly backs towards the Gate. Her gaze never leaves me, her weapon steady and unmoving. Waves of fear crash over me. My mind screams for action, but my body is paralysed with fear. I know deep down that there is no stopping her now, no matter what I do.

"Please," I croak in a shaky voice. "Don't leave me here." I can't stop the tears as I realise the hopelessness of the situation.

She looks sad and shakes her head slowly.

"Goodbye Becky," she whispers, and steps backwards through the Gate.

A guttural, unintelligible animal noise of anguish erupts from my throat as I stumble towards the Gate. My heart pounds in my chest as I reach for the black disc, only to watch it disappear before my eyes.

It's gone.

Trapped and helpless, I collapse to my knees and bury my head in my arms, tears streaming down my face as sobs wrack my body uncontrollably. The overwhelming sense of despair and hopelessness envelopes me, weighing me down like a heavy cloak.

This is my fate now; trapped in a world I never wanted to be a part of.

The Parasite

I know I'm going to die.

It's inevitable, and it's my fault.

I lie on my side in the tall grass, unable to move. I can only blink, breathe and twitch the fingers of my right hand, and soon I won't be able to do that. Soon, the poison will have run its course, and my breathing will stop.

I curse myself and my stupidity once more. It took just two days. Two days of searching and finding nothing for me to make my fatal mistake. As I watch, the undergrowth in front of me rustles and the long grass sways. It's probably a predator.

There is no pain. It's one of the few things left I can do. Ten minutes ago, I accessed the pain centres in my brain and turned them off. A simple thing that an Assisted telepath like me can do. The device I'm wearing gives me control over areas of my mind. Like memories, involuntary reactions, emotions and, of course, pain.

As soon as the snake struck, I knew I was in trouble. It was big, with green and yellow stripes. I stood on its tail, and it reared up, striking and biting me in the thigh. It wasn't interested in me. I had startled it and it had struck out in self-defence. As my leg turned numb and I fell to my knees, I watched it slither away. The poison was fast acting, much faster than I expected and, I think, much faster than snakes in my world.

The rustling is closer now. Whatever approaches it's not big. There's nothing I can do to escape. I can only hope that I'm dead before whatever it is starts chewing on my flesh.

I should have been more careful, but I had grown desperate and therefore thrown caution to the proverbial wind. How could I have known that finding my way back to my world would be so difficult?

I blink rapidly and try once more to move. It's no use, my muscles are paralysed. The tall grass in front of me parts and something slides towards me. It's black, and glides like a slug over the ground. Three thin, snake-like tentacles writhe in the air before it as it tastes and feels its way towards me. Part of me is relieved. It's not a predator. It doesn't have claws or teeth. Another part of me is disgusted by the slimy thing.

Soon, the thing becomes completely exposed, and it's only two feet away from my face. It has a tail that is made up of what looks like lots of thin, long, black hairs. They wave back and forth as foot long slug approaches.

Maybe it intends to digest me with its digestive juices, or maybe I'm just lying in its path, and it will go around or over me. Either way, I can do nothing. By now, I can feel my breathing falter as the poison continues its inexorable path.

The slug is at my face. I can feel its tentacles caress my cheek. It seems to be searching for something. If I could, I would brush the thing away, but I can't. It doesn't take long for it to find my nose where it pushes all three of its tentacles up a nostril.

It moves forward and terror hits me as I realise that its black body is elongating and it's pushing forward. It's going to eat me from the inside!

I lie helpless as it slides into my nose. I pray that the poison takes me before it starts eating. There is still no pain, but I can feel it propelling itself up to the base of my nose, and then the terror strikes me anew as I hear a crunching. The horrible thing is eating its way into my brain!

Surely the poison will take me soon, and death will spare me from this new horror.

The crunching has stopped. My breathing has slowed. It won't be long now. I feel blood trickle from my nose and drip onto the ground before me. I can feel pressure in my head. It moves to the rear of my skull where it stops, and all is still. Has it found what it wants to eat?

My chest grows tight and spasms as my body struggles to breathe. Not long now. I'm relieved. I don't want to experience the slug thing eating my brain. My vision darkens. I wish I hadn't started on my journey in the first place. I should have listened to Rithvik my brother.

"There's no way Inaya!" he had told me. "You won't be able to find her. You don't know where she went. You don't know which world she'll be in. It's like finding a needle in a haystack!"

Of course, I ignored him. I would do anything to find her. She was the love of my life. I would cross oceans to be with her. Of course, I didn't actually cross oceans, instead I travelled to other worlds, following and searching. My brother was right. I didn't find her. And now I wasn't going to. My search was at an end. I was going to die here in this world.

Suddenly, without warning, my foot twitches. My vision grows brighter and my breathing eases.

What's this? I should be dead. Instead, I can move the toes on my left foot. I don't understand and am surprised when suddenly control returns to the muscles in my face and I'm able to frown. I lick my lips slowly and deliberately, tasting the blood from my nose.

I wait helplessly as my limb's spasm and jerk; the muscles coming back to life.

After a few minutes, I'm able to sit up.

I just sit in the grass, breathing and waiting for the pins and needles in my legs to go. I wipe my nose with the back of my hand and stare at the blood. The thing is still inside me. I might have recovered from the poison, but the thing was still inside my head. Why aren't I dead? It makes no sense. One moment my life was ebbing away, the next I was sitting up, examining blood on my hand.

I'm not sure what to do. Somehow, I've escaped death, although, has it merely been delayed? The slug in my head was probably gorging right now. I've grown careless. There's been no sign of Clarissa and I'm lost. I travelled through many worlds to get to this one. I wasn't sure how to get back.

What was that? I can hear something.

"*You're mine,*" the voice whispers.

I know I didn't hear it with my ears. I'm a telepath. I know the difference between sound and thought. The voice is in my head. I put two and two together.

"*You're the slug,*" I think clearly and with practised ease.

"*Slug is derogatory, I am a Braxis,*" the voice whispers.

"*What's a Braxis? And what are you doing in my head?*" I'm not sure I want to know the answer.

"*The Braxis are the supreme race. We rule everywhere and everything.*"

The voice is quiet. I can only just hear it. But it is arrogant and confident. Dread and fear fill me. An alien thing has crawled into my brain. Somehow, it's connected with me and can communicate. Why, I don't know. Was this just the prelude to it chomping away? Eating me from the inside?

"*Why are you in my head? Are you going to eat me?*" I ask, but I don't really want the answer.

"*I will not kill you,*" the quiet voice replies.

At first, I am relieved.

"*You neutralised the snake poison?*" I stated, not really asking.

"*Yes.*"

"How?"

"I am connected to your intravenous system. It is a simple matter to secrete the antidote."

"But why?"

"A dead host is no use to me. I need you alive."

I consider its words. I don't like the way the conversation is going. My initial fear retreats a little. At least it isn't going to kill me, but I have a bad feeling about the situation.

"Then what?" I ask. "What is your intention?"

"You are my host. Through your thoughts, I can see that you possess the ability to traverse between worlds. Until this point, the Braxis have been confined solely to this world. With your help, we will expand our reach to other worlds where we will conquer and reign."

A terrifying thought grows inside me. Understanding hits me like a hammer blow. I can't believe how stupid I've been. The slug is a parasite. It must use other animals as living hosts. What a horrible thing, and now it thinks that it can use me to travel to other worlds. I grit my teeth in determination. I couldn't allow that. Somehow, I had to get rid of it.

"You can't get rid of me," it replies. "I am with you until your death."

I pause. Obviously, it can hear my thoughts. I remember the thin hairs waving in the air at its rear end as it approached me. I now realise that they are nerve fibres. It's probably threading them and interfacing with my brain right now. I'm repulsed as I imagine the hairs worming their way through my grey matter. Just how far would that connection go? Would it allow the Braxis to influence me? Maybe even to control me? Would it even be able to move my limbs, making me a passenger in my body?

"You are perceptive. It is pleasing to reside within an intelligent host," the voice whispers in my head.

I have to do something. I can't allow this thing to stay in my head, to manipulate and control me. Worse, I can't allow it to travel to my world. The thought of it invading the bodies of my family and friends fills me with horror. But what can I do?

The pins and needles have gone, as has all the numbness. I gaze around where I sit. The long grass comes up to my shoulders. Trees form a line a few metres away. Behind me, the grass stretches out on an endless plain. There is nothing here.

Slowly, a plan starts to form in my head. But I can't think about it or the Braxis will know what I intend to do. I must distract it as well as myself. I must not think.

"What happened to your last host?" I ask as I struggle, unsteadily to my feet.

"My last host was a stupid animal. It died."

I walk towards the distant tree line, concentrating on questions I can ask the Braxis.

"Is there no intelligent life in this world?"

"No longer," is the whispered answer. "They all died."

I approach the trees. I select one with long thin branches that I can reach.

"Why did they all die?" I ask.
"It is taxing for animals to host us. We exert a significant toll on their bodies. Many do not last more than a year."

Jesus Christ! I can't help the thought. This thing was going to suck the life out of me! I break off the short dead branch. It has a sharp point.

"How many hosts have you had?"

"I have had many hosts in my lifetime. I cannot count them all."

I take a deep breath.

"STOP!" The Braxis shouts in my mind.

It has learned what I intend to do. I must act quickly. I don't know how much time I have. Before long, it might control me and make me stop.

I bring up the dead branch and ram the sharp end into my neck.

There is no pain save for the screaming thing in my head as it rages and wails at what I have done. I collapse to the ground. Blood sprays from my neck where I have severed my carotid artery.

I lie on my side, my life ebbing away. I'll never find my Clarissa. But I have no regrets. I've foiled the Braxis, but at a high price. I'm back on the ground. My lifeblood seeps into the surrounding grass. Inside my head the Braxis wails and shrieks. I smile grimly. I'm going to die in this world after all.

The Mistake

"You idiot!" she spat at me. "Why did you revive me?"

I was taken-a-back. I thought I'd done a good thing. After all, she'd nearly died.

"You've killed me!" she exclaimed. "You're medalling with things you don't understand!"

I couldn't answer. What was she talking about? I had just saved her life. She should be thanking me.

"You bloody fool!" she continued with her rant. "How long have I been out of my tank?"

Before I could answer, she continued.

"Don't tell me, it doesn't matter!" she looked around the room from her prone position. "I'm dead, anyway!"

There was anger and hate all over her face as she turned her head away from me and spat over the side of her suspension chamber onto the floor. She actually spat. It was disgusting.

I was still speechless. Her behaviour had taken me completely by surprise. What was wrong with her? I watched as she struggled to raise herself up to pull herself out of the chamber. I somehow couldn't bring myself to help her. Instead, I stood there, dumb, as she flopped around, her hands slipping on the chamber sides, the preserving liquid splashing over her naked body.

She cursed and grumbled to herself. Realising that she couldn't get out on her own, her dark eyes cut over to me.

"Get me out of here, you moron!" she griped at me.

Her sharp tone of voice broke me out of my inactivity, and I stepped forward. She gripped my arm with her cold, wet hand and pulled herself up. She noticed me averting my gaze as she rose and stepped out; the liquid cascading over her body and dripping onto the floor.

"What's the matter?" she snarled. "Bet you had a good long look when I was asleep."

She was right, of course. I'd spent a long time admiring her curves and the serene expression on her face. But that was then. Now that she was awake, it was clear to me that she was a horrible person. It seems that looks are not everything after all.

I strode away to an open locker on against the wall, pulled out a folded white towel and threw it back at her. She caught it deftly and unashamedly turned her attention to drying herself off.

I turned and faced the lockers, trying to make sense of the situation. Just a few hours ago I had travelled to this world. I had hoped the journey to be one of discovery, but from the very first moment, as I had walked through the portal and stepped into this parallel universe, everything had gone wrong.

First, I noticed the lack of people. The streets were eerily quiet and devoid of any life, though there was still evidence of animals with many birds, insects, dogs, and cats. Houses stood abandoned, with some being boarded-up windows and doors. The once bustling shops and businesses had been ransacked; glass shards littered the ground. Random items were scattered everywhere, making it difficult to navigate on foot. I ended up walking down the middle of the road, carefully avoiding abandoned cars with open doors as if their owners had left in a hurry.

Then there were the signs.

They were unmissable, written with red paint and in giant letters on the sides of buildings. They were everywhere.

SAVE YOURSELF - SLEEP

SLEEP TO LIVE

THE FUTURE IS OURS

TODAY IS LOST

They were all similar, seemingly encouraging people to sleep themselves into the future. But why? Were they slogans used by the local government or the police?

And finally, there was this complex. I use the term loosely because it's more than just a single structure; it's a fully functioning world within a world. A small, unassuming building held an elevator that descended deep into the ground beneath the empty city. As I explored, I discovered medical facilities, living quarters, restaurants, and workspaces scattered throughout the vast underground expanse. It was truly immense.

And then, just when I thought there was nothing left to find, I stumbled into the lowest level, and was shocked to find all the people that had gone missing - they were all sealed away in what were obviously some kind of life suspension chambers.

There were rows and rows of them in room after room after room. There must have been thousands of unconscious people. At that moment, I realised what the signs meant, but why? Why would these people willingly allow themselves to be put into these chambers? Presumably to be revived at some point in the future, but when? None of it made sense.

Sometime later, as I wandered up and down the halls of sleeping people, I found a small room that contained just one suspension chamber and, inside, lay the most beautiful woman I had ever seen.

I couldn't take my eyes off her. Like all the others, she lay completely naked, her long blonde hair waving gently in the transparent liquid that circulated around her body. There was something about her that registered with me on a subconscious level. I felt a connection, something intangible, something that I had never felt before.

It was ridiculous. She was unconscious, not aware of her surroundings. How could I feel such a strong connection with such powerful emotions? It didn't make any sense.

"Snap out of it!" she shouted at my back. "Make yourself useful and pass me some clothes from locker twenty-four."

I turned to see her standing, the damp towel at her feet and her arms crossed in front of her. Try as I might, I couldn't stop my eyes from dropping to her breasts and then to her thighs.

She glared at me, noticing the focus of my gaze. I flushed and turned back to the lockers. It took me a moment to locate number twenty-four. I wrenched open the door and reached inside to grab a plastic box containing a neat bundle of clothes. As I turned back to her, I was startled to find her right next to me. Her bare feet had made no noise as she had approached.

She grabbed the box from me, her bright green eyes still full of anger.

"For fuck's sake!" she exclaimed.

I could feel her hot breath on my face as she continued to scold me.

"Get on with it! Or do you want me to stay naked?"

I let her take the box from me and turned away once again, trying desperately to get my thoughts together. This wasn't like me. Normally, I was in control and knew what to do, no matter the situation. I was usually loud and outspoken, yet here I was, acting like some dumb teenager. I needed to pull myself together quickly and find out what was going on. Why was she so angry? What was her reason for claiming that I had killed her? Why were these people in suspended animation? What was happening in this world?

"Where did you come from?" she asked from behind me. "Why aren't you sleeping with the rest? Or did your tank malfunction?"

From the tone of her voice, I could tell that she had calmed down a little.

"I'm not from here," I answered. I remained facing away from her.

"What do you mean?" she asked. "Are you from another sector?"

Sector? What was she talking about? Should I tell her the truth? I figured I had nothing to lose.

"I'm not from your world," I replied.

"Bollocks!" she scoffed. "Did you somehow evade the round-up teams?"

What was a round-up team? That sounded ominous.

"No, I travelled from a world parallel to this one. I'm a researcher."

There was the sound of a zip being pulled.

"Turn around and say that to my face, you liar!"

I did as asked and once again was struck by her beauty. Her blonde hair was still slightly damp and tousled, evidence of her efforts to dry it. She wore a short white skirt with a daring slit up the side, paired with white trainers and a fitted powder blue top that accentuated her curves.

She rolled her eyes.

"When you've stopped ogling, maybe you can answer my question? This time without lying?"

I flushed once again.

"It's true," I told her. "I've travelled here from another world."

She just shook her head. She pushed past me and reached into the open locker that had contained her clothes. Her hand came out with a packet of cigarettes and a lighter.

She eyed me over her hands as she lit up.

"I don't know why I'm bothering to ask," she blew smoke towards me. I wafted it away with my hands. She stood with her elbow on her hip, a wisp of smoke curling towards the ceiling from the cigarette smoking in her hand.

"The display on your, er, tank was flashing an error when I found you," I explained. "The display told me to press the red button to save your life."

I watched her eyes narrow into thin slits as she inhaled from her cigarette again.

"And truthfully," I continued. "I really am from another world. I'm sorry if I did the wrong thing, I was just following instructions. I thought I was saving you."

She snorted.

"Well, let me tell you, whoever you are. Far from saving me, you've killed me! Oh, and by the way, you're dead too!"

I frowned. She was talking in riddles. There was silence between us as she puffed on her cigarette, never taking her eyes from me.

"What are you talking about?" I asked. "You're not dead. I saved you!"

She grimaced, threw the cigarette to the floor and stamped on it. She turned away and strode out of the room. I hesitated for a brief second and followed.

She was a total mystery. Confident, outspoken, and full of herself. Yet she carried herself with a beauty and sensuality that couldn't be denied. I was captivated by her.

I followed her out of the room and found her gazing at the rows of suspension chambers, or "tanks" as she called them. I stood beside her, trying to understand what was happening.

"At least they have a chance," she whispered to herself.

"A chance at what?" I asked.

She glanced up at me, anger in her eyes once more.

"At life, you moron! Unlike us, they'll live."

She took out another cigarette from the packet and lit up again.

"You keep talking about death and dying, but we're still here," I pointed out. "Very much alive."

As she drew in a lungful of smoke, a look of pity flickered across her face.

"You really don't know, do you?" she asked.

I shook my head. "Like I said, I'm a visitor. I've no idea what you're talking about."

She didn't answer. Instead, she turned back to face the rows of tanks, blowing out smoke in big white plumes.

I waited for her to explain, admiring the way her damp hair cascaded over her shoulders. Eventually, she spoke up.

"This facility is one of many," her voice taking on a lecturing tone. "They're all designed to save as many of the population as possible." She turned to face me. "Did you notice anything unusual up there?" she gestured towards the ceiling.

"Not really," I answered. "Apart from there being no one around." I nodded to the rows of tanks. "Now I see that everyone was down here."

"Nothing?" she asked, her eyebrows arching.

I thought back to when I was walking through the empty streets and shook my head.

"The sky?" she asked.

She took one final drag from her cigarette before crushing it against the rough concrete beneath her feet. I furrowed my brow in confusion, trying to make sense of what she was saying.

"If you'd bothered to look up," she continued. "You would have seen it."

I frowned harder, my eyebrows drawing together.

She sighed and folded her arms.

"The comet. You didn't see the comet?"

I shook my head once again. I still had no clue what she was talking about.

"You must be blind!" she said contemptuously. "It must be filling the sky by now!"

"I saw nothing in the sky," I replied. "Admittedly, I wasn't actually looking up. I was walking through the city, but if there was something up there, I'm pretty sure I would have seen it."

It was her turn to frown. Her eyebrows bunched together, and dimples appeared in her cheeks as she pouted, clearly confused. I thought she looked even more adorable.

"Maybe it's on the other side of the world," she murmured to herself.

As if on cue, the ground trembled and a low rumble reverberated through the vast room. My head whipped around to survey the area. I quickly scanned the vast room, noticing small puffs of dust swirling around the nearby tanks and fine particles falling from the ceiling.

There was silence as we both looked at each other, then the silence was broken by a shrieking alarm. Before I could ask what was going on, I heard another sound. It was a slow grinding noise that sounded as though something very heavy was being dragged along the floor.

"What the hell is that?" I asked.

She stood there silently before responding. The grinding noise suddenly ceased with a loud boom and the blaring alarm abruptly cut off, leaving behind an eerie silence that seemed almost as deafening as the alarm itself.

"It's the airtight doors, sealing the tomb."

My eyes went wide, and I drew in a quick, sharp breath.

"Tomb?"

"Haven't you worked out where we are yet?" she asked scornfully.

"How could I? All you've done is shout at me since I saved your life!" I was starting to get angry.

"You didn't save me, you killed me!" she hissed at me, her eyes slits, her mouth sneering.

"You already said that," I retorted, my voice getting louder. I needed to know what was going on. "But you haven't explained how. All I did was follow the instructions on your tank!"

"So you say," she snapped. "I only have your word for that!"

"It's true," I told her, exasperated. "Why else would I revive you?"

She looked me up and down, contempt on her face, and raised her eyebrows.

"There could be any number of reasons why, some more obvious than others."

She brushed past me, making her way back to the room containing her tank. I blew the air out of my lungs in annoyance. The situation was ridiculous. Things were not getting clearer. I watched the dust from the ceiling settle around the suspension chambers for a while, considering my options. I could just leave. Obviously, I couldn't open a portal to my world from here - there was no such complex as this in my world, so it would open into rock. I would have to make my way back up to the surface. But how deep were we? I wasn't sure. On the way down, the lift seemed to travel for quite a while. I concluded we must be several hundred metres down. That was a problem. I raised my right arm and gazed at the rings on my fingers that made up my Assist. It was a marvel of micro-engineering that boosted my mental faculties, amongst other things. With it, I could open portals to other worlds and teleport across vast distances. But I couldn't teleport through hundreds of metres of rock. I needed to get back to the surface. My Assist might be a marvel of engineering, but it had its limits.

I sighed and retraced my steps, returning to the small room we had just left. To my surprise, it was empty. Where had she gone? Then I spied another door at the back of the room. I must have overlooked it earlier; but then, my attention had been fixated on the body in the suspension chamber. A rueful smile crossed my face as I remembered her nakedness.

As I approached the chamber, I paused to inspect the small control panel on its side. Had I made a mistake? It told me to press the red button, didn't it? Surely, I couldn't have mis-read it? Could I?

Sure enough, the panel was flashing red and was displaying the words:

MALFUNCTION: END STASIS.

I breathed a sigh of relief. I was right. I shouldn't have doubted myself. I was about to turn away when I noticed more lettering beneath the display:

DR CATHERINE 'CAT' MILFORD (PRIORITY A).

So, her name was Cat. Somewhat appropriate, I thought to myself as I walked into the second room. She was certainly displaying some cat characteristics!

She surprised me yet again. I'm not sure what I expected to find, but I was not expecting to see her lounging and relaxed on a sofa with a cigarette in one hand and a glass of something that looked alcoholic in the other.

As I entered, her gaze flicked to me and then moved away as she took a pull from her cigarette and then a sip from her drink. She looked back at me blowing smoke in my direction; her drink clinking gently with ice.

Her beauty stunned me once again. I wasn't a fan of smoking, but she somehow made it look alluring as she sat with her legs crossed, revealing a lot of thigh.

I cleared my throat.

"I just checked. Your tank did malfunction. The error message is still displayed. I definitely saved you."

She stared at me; the smoke curling upwards from her cigarette; the ice clinking as she swirled her tumbler.

"I know," she answered eventually.

"You do?" I asked.

She nodded.

"I checked. Oh, don't think I'm grateful. You should have left me, at least then I wouldn't feel anything. Now, thanks to you, I'm destined to know that I'm going to die!"

The ungrateful bitch! I had saved her, and she wasn't thankful at all! I couldn't believe it. I needed to disregard my attraction to her. She was, as I had already surmised, a monster.

"So, are you going to tell me what's going on here?" I asked.

She swirled her tumbler some more, appearing to consider my request. Then she sighed.

"Alright, I'll indulge you, though I'm sure that you're pulling my leg or messing me about for some reason."

She took another sip from her drink.

"As you no doubt know, about ten years ago, astronomers spotted a comet heading towards the inner solar system. They said that while it wouldn't hit Earth, it would come close, too close. They said that it would have a devastating effect."

She put her cigarette to her mouth and drew in a lungful of smoke. She looked sideways at me and then tipped her head back, blowing smoke up at the ceiling.

"The gravitational pull would tear away the atmosphere and trigger massive earthquakes. All living things would perish. So, we did the only thing possible. We dug. We constructed lots of underground citadels, inside of which, as you have seen, all our population were placed in suspended animation, to be revived once the world above recovered and it was safe for them to emerge."

She took another sip, finishing the contents of her glass, and directed a piercing gaze at me, waiting for my reaction. However, before I could respond, a thunderous noise erupted, and the room trembled violently, causing me to stagger. I reached out to a wall to steady myself. Everything went quiet. I looked around warily. Over on the sofa, Cat was staring at me. I wasn't sure what to say. Her explanation didn't sound plausible to me. Oh sure, it explained why everyone was in the suspension chambers, but I had seen no evidence of a comet as I'd walked through the abandoned city. But then again, there was the rumbling and shaking. Only something big could cause that.

I cleared my throat and was about to reply when she suddenly threw the empty glass at me. Fortunately, I'm blessed with fast reflexes, because her aim was true. If I hadn't ducked in time, it would have hit me on the forehead. As it was, it missed and smashed against the wall.

"And now, because of you, I'm going to die!" she screamed at me.

I'd had enough. That was the final straw. I was getting out. There were plenty of other worlds to explore.

"I don't care anymore," I told her. "I haven't done anything wrong. I don't deserve your contempt. I'm leaving."

She spluttered and then laughed.

"You dumb ass, you aren't going anywhere," she said once she could control herself. "Like I said, the tomb is sealed."

It was my turn to sneer.

"Locked doors can't stop me." I waved a hand at her. "You stay here and rot if you want, but I'm going."

I turned and started walking to the doorway.

"The door has an electronic lock that's disabled. It won't open no matter what you do." She called after me.

I didn't bother to reply, instead I kept walking. I didn't care anymore. I'd had enough of her sniping and nasty comments.

"Wait!" she shouted as I entered the suspension chamber hall. I heard her footsteps as she ran to catch me. Her hand grabbed my arm and spun me around.

"You can't get out!" she spat at me.

I gently removed her hand and continued towards the exit.

"You can't get out!" she shouted again from behind me.

I ignored her and continued towards the exit. As I expected, Cat was correct. A sturdy steel door obstructed the entrance, resembling the type you would find in a secure nuclear bunker. Its sheer size and weight indicated that it was designed to safeguard the large number of people sleeping in the hall behind me. It wouldn't present a problem. I could recall the layout of the underground complex. I knew where I could teleport to on the other side of this door.

"Wait!" Cat shouted again from behind me. "What are you going to do?"

I looked over my shoulder as she approached.

"I'm going to teleport to the other side," I answered. It was her turn to look confused. I raised my right hand and jangled the chains of my Assist by wriggling my fingers. "With this."

Her gaze snapped from my eyes to my hand and then back again. Something flickered across her face. Was it doubt? Or was it hope?

"You're not joking?" she asked. I was sure I detected a hint of eagerness in her voice.

I shook my head. Her look of confusion changed back to the familiar sneer. She didn't believe me. I shrugged, raised my right hand, and flexed my fingers. In a snap, I was on the other side of the bunker door.

All I had to do was make my way up to the surface. I assumed that there would be no power for the lift, which would make my exit awkward. I would have to teleport up through the levels one by one. Fortunately, my Assist gave me an eidetic memory. I would know exactly where it was safe to 'port' to. I would be out of here and back in my world in ten minutes.

I walked away from the door, but then paused. I couldn't leave Cat to die on the other side of the door. My shoulders slumped and my head dropped. I sighed deeply. For fuck's sake! I would have to go back and get her. Even though she had been nothing but horrible to me, I couldn't leave her to die.

I raised my hand once more and 'ported' back into the suspension hall.

I was surprised to find Cat sitting on the floor with her back against the wall, her knees up and her head in her hands.

As soon as I arrived, she looked up with tear-filled eyes. She'd been crying.

My heart melted. I said nothing, just held out my hand. Her eyes locked on mine and didn't waver as she stood and walked over. She took my hand and smiled uncertainly. Pulling her to me, I slid my hand around her waist and flicked my fingers. Together, we 'ported' to the other side of the door.

It wasn't long before we were in my world.

Much later, after we'd spent some time together, I couldn't resist asking her: "Do you still think I made a mistake reviving you?"

She looked at me with a smile on her face and reached up to caress my cheek.

"It was the best mistake you ever made," she declared before standing on her toes, leaning in, and planting a kiss on my lips.

Madness

I've gone mad!

Quite literally stark raving bonkers!

I see things. Bright colours streaming and bouncing around my flat. I see them even through my tightly closed eyelids.

I hear things. I hear people arguing and chatting; I hear whispers, shouting and yelling. All of it with my hands over my ears.

I feel things. I feel emotions that aren't my own. I feel anger and despair, desire and hunger. Even though I'm on my own.

I can't cope; I'm overloaded with stuff, data, things, and thoughts. I groan and writhe on the bed. Nothing helps; nothing stops the overload. It feels like an assault, as though these voices, lights and emotions are being pushed into my mind from the outside, but of course, I know that's not possible. So, it's obvious that I've gone mad.

Eventually, I rise from the bed, stagger into the small kitchenette, and grab a glass from a cupboard above the worktop. I fill it with water from the cold tap and drain it in one. A woman's scream causes me to snap my head around, searching for the owner of that piercing yell, but there is nothing there.

Striding over to the flat window, I peer into the floodlit street. It's empty save for parked cars that line both sides of the road. The owner of the shriek isn't there. It's in my head! The scream is in my head!

I've surely gone mad; there can be no other explanation.

I sit on the side of the bed and try to decide what to do. Eyes closed, head in my hands, I try to think. It's almost impossible. There's so much distraction with the colours and the voices. A sudden flare of anger hits me, making me gasp, but it's immediately replaced by a wave of sexual desire so intense that it leaves me breathless. As soon as these foreign emotions arrive, they disappear, leaving a void where my own emotions crash into themselves. I feel fear and puzzlement in equal measure. What is happening to me?

I must do something, but what? Should I go to Accident and Emergency? Confess what was happening to me? But if I do, I will surely sound like a madwoman. Why would anyone believe me? No, I can't go to A&E; they wouldn't be able to help.

I stand quickly. Slipping out of my pyjamas, I pull on my running joggers and shoes with a T-shirt. I have to do something; I just don't know what, so I do the only thing I can. I grab my keys from the table and exit the flat. I race down the stairs, my footsteps echoing and providing a backdrop beat to the thrum of voices in my head.

Outside, it's cold and dark; the only light comes from the streetlights. I turn right and run, my blonde hair trailing behind me in the wind as I pound down the pavement. I feel as though I'm running from the voices, but fresh voices speak in my head as I run while others fade to nothing.

Vibrant colours flow and stream from the dark houses as I run past them, some so bright that I wave my hand in front of my face in a futile effort to brush them away. More emotions crash into my brain, some overpowering. One minute, I find tears running down my face as I mourn a lost partner I've never had. The next, I laugh, elated as I win a card game I've never played.

It's all so confusing and frightening. I've lost control, and I don't know what's happening. I'm running and breathing hard, trying to escape, but there is no escape. I can't control myself; I throw back my head and howl into the air. I don't stop running. I scream and race down the road as fast as I can.

It's not long before I can't go any further; my lungs are burning, and I can't get enough oxygen. I double over, gasping and wheezing, my hands on my knees. It takes a few minutes before I recover and realise something has changed.

The voices are quieter; the colours are dimmer and the emotions more distant. Finally, I can think. Nearby, there is a wooden bench. I walk over to it and sit, my elbows on my knees and my hands clasped before me.

I take deep, slow breaths, and I feel calmer. I tightly clasp my hands together, sighing with relief as I feel the hard and smooth rings on my fingers. Absently, I play with the tiny chains connecting the rings while I try to make sense of what just happened. The now muted colours spiral around in the air before me, and the voices are whispering instead of shouting. What is wrong with me? It makes no sense; I don't understand.

A voice startles me from my thoughts.

"Where did you get that?" asks a deep masculine voice with a calm confidence.

I am shocked to see a man wearing a long black coat sitting at the other end of the bench. He wasn't there before; where did he come from? I can't see his face; his coat has a hood, which shadows his features.

Fear surges, and adrenalin flows in my veins, making my legs shake. I left the flat without my phone or my personal alarm. I feel vulnerable. All I have on are my thin joggers and T-shirt, and I'm alone out in the middle of the night.

"The rings, I mean." The stranger spoke again.

I look back at my rings. They're new and unique. I've never seen anything like them - five gold rings, each connected to the other with a tiny gold chain.

The man is going to rob me, I'm sure of it. I stand quickly, intending to run.

"Don't go," says the man, his voice as calm as anything.

I hesitate, then speed away, back the way I came, the adrenalin giving me a boost of energy. I look back over my shoulder as I run. The stranger isn't following. He sits unmoving and still.

I heave a sigh of relief and keep running back towards my flat. But as I run, the voices come back with a vengeance, screaming and wailing between my ears. The colours flare brightly, causing me to squint, and the emotions pile back in on top of each other, hammering at my thoughts.

I falter and miss a step, stumbling on the pavement and almost fall. I reach out a hand to steady myself and find it grasped in a grip like iron that stops me from falling.

I mumble my thanks as I try to see my saviour through half-closed eyelids and the bright, shimmering coloured light.

"I'd like to help if you'd let me," says a voice I instantly recognise.

I pull my hand back in shock and step backwards. I blink up at a smiling face half hidden by his hood. Fear hits me once again, and my eyes widen in shock. The light hurts my eyes even more. I can't process what I see. He's here, standing next to me. It's impossible. He can't be here. Does he have a twin?

For a few seconds, my mouth opens and closes like a goldfish. My head hurts. The voices shriek and the colours blaze. I'm dazed and confused.

"It's okay, Sarah, I can help." Says the stranger.

I clamp my mouth shut as the fear takes over. I don't think I just act. I turn and run as fast as I can once more. I'm gasping and sucking in the cold air. My leg muscles hurt, and my mind screams - stop, but I don't.

I collapse at the steps up to my flat. I can't go on, I can't breathe. My head throbs with the most painful headache I've ever had. Lights flowing around the stairway blind me; the emotions that aren't mine crash into my own, leaving me disorientated and bewildered. The cacophony of voices scream and shout. I can't marshal my thoughts. My mind turns to mush, my vision narrows, and I sink into oblivion.

I awake suddenly. The first thing I notice is the quiet and stillness. The voices are gone, as are the coloured lights, and there are no foreign emotions hammering at my brain. The relief is palpable. Then I become aware I'm lying on my back in my bed.

At first, I'm baffled about how and why I got here, but then I hear the soft clink of metal coming from my left. I turn my head to see the stranger sitting comfortably in a chair, his legs crossed, my new rings dangling from his hand.

Realisation dawns on me. He's in my flat! He knows my name! He's a stalker! He's going to kill me! I roll to my right, away from the stranger, and fall to the floor. I scrabble to my feet and press myself against the wall on the far side of the bed. My heart thuds in my chest. I'm scared, and I clutch my hands to my chest. My breathing is rapid and gasping.

"Where did you get these?" the stranger asks again, holding out my rings.

I don't answer; my eyes dart around the room and settle on my phone. It's on the table near the stranger.

The stranger sighs and pulls back his hood, revealing a handsome face with long blond hair. He has bright, almost luminous blue eyes.

"You can't hear the voices because I've removed these rings." He grasps them in his hand. "You're obviously very sensitive and need training."

I don't answer. I have no idea what he's talking about, and I don't care. I calculate the distance to the table. Can I get to the phone and call for help?

"You have a choice to make." The stranger continues. "You can stay as you are," he surveyed my flat with dispassionate eyes. He can't disguise a look of distaste. "Or you can put these rings back on and come with me."

I don't know how to respond. I don't want to answer. I want him to go away. I want to be on my own. How does he know my name? My gaze flits over to the door. I can't reach my phone, but maybe I can get to the door.

"Don't run again," the stranger says. He stands in one quick, fluid movement. "I'll make it easy for you."

I press my back against the wall.

"I'm taking this," he gestures with his closed fist. "If you want to learn more, you can find me at this address."

He reaches into a pocket and pulls out a small card, which he places on the table next to my phone. He stares at me for a brief second, then turns and exits my flat.

Relief floods over me like a tidal wave. My shoulders sag, and I blow out a lungful of air.

Then I smile and walk to the table to pick up my phone. I dial a number and wait for someone to pick up.

"Is it done?" asks the voice.

"Yes," I reply.

"Well, done. I knew you could do it. Does he suspect anything?"

"No, it was easy, apart from those rings. They were a bitch!"

The voice chuckled.

"Yes, they take some getting used to."

"A warning would have helped!" I complain.

"Half the money has been transferred. You'll receive the remaining half once you confirm his death."

I disconnect the call. I pull a backpack from under the bed, throw it over my shoulder, and pick up the stranger's business card. I walk past the table and leave the flat forever.

Discarded

Have you ever fallen in love with a telepath? I have, and let me tell you, it's not all that it's cracked up to be.

In fact, it's hell.

Academically, you'd think that it would be a good thing. You could communicate without speech, which, presumably, would be faster and more efficient. You'd know everything about each other. You'd know, without a shadow of a doubt, that he really loved you, if he cheated on you or if he found someone else attractive. You'd never be lied to, because you would know you'd be able to tell.

It sounds perfect, right?

Well, let me tell you, it's not.

Of course, no one believes me, not even here. Oh, I have a friend who says she does, but does she? Does she really?

That's the first problem with falling in love with a telepath. They don't exist, so how could anyone possibly believe anything you say about them?

The second problem is that it's all one way. That is, if he's the telepath and you're not, then he knows everything, and you know nothing. You're just the dumb, blind shmuck who's a lower form of life. An un-evolved ape incapable of feeling or reading other people's emotions, thoughts, or feelings. You're down there in the gutter with all the other blind apes destined to stay there for the rest of your life, while he's an elevated being. He's a thing of beauty, a thing to be admired, to revere and to lust over.

Do I sound bitter? You would too, if it had happened to you.

It started just two weeks ago. At the time, I was a respected and brilliant teacher at a secondary school. Well, others thought I was brilliant. They had no idea that I was constantly on the back foot, creating my lesson plans at the last minute, working long hours just to keep ahead of all the marking. It was a vicious treadmill that I couldn't get off. I was good at putting on a front, of making my colleagues think I was in control. The truth was, I was on the edge. The knife edge of success and failure. There's no way I would choose to teach as a career if I could do things over.

It was the weekend, and as usual, I was working. I had a batch of assignments to mark and the week's lessons to plan. As I often do, I like a change of scenery, so I left my tiny flat and drove to a nearby Costa, where I sat in front of my laptop with a hot cappuccino.

The staff were used to me. I'd been here many times before. They didn't mind me sitting in the corner. The place was never busy, and they seemed to be content to let me stay as long as I wanted, which was usually three or four hours.

I'd nearly finished the marking when he walked in.

I noticed him straight away. There was something about him, something undefinable. It could have been the self-assured walk, the casualness of his smile or the confidence in his voice as he ordered his drink at the counter. Whatever it was, it got him noticed, and not just by me. The young girl behind the display was clearly flustered. Her face was red, and I could see her hand shaking as she handed over his coffee.

I was just as bad. I couldn't take my eyes off him, my work forgotten, as he walked to a nearby table and sat. I watched as he sipped his drink and pulled a newspaper from his shoulder bag. He was like a magnet for my eyes, and it took an effort of will to tear my gaze away to refocus on the laptop screen.

Of course, I couldn't concentrate. It was hopeless. For the next half hour, I typed nonsense into my laptop while taking furtive glances across at the stranger. Eventually I gave up and closed the laptop's lid and sighed to myself. The situation was ridiculous. I'm not some sixteen-year-old girl. I'm a mature woman of thirty-one. I'd had my share of lovers. Why was I acting like this? Why was he affecting me so much?

I couldn't let this go on. I had work to do, so I packed my bag with my notes and exited the premises, all the while steeling myself not to look back.

The following week was one of boredom, stress and an impossible workload. I was glad when the weekend came round again. As usual, I had a mountain of work to do, as I did every weekend. But this time I was determined to get it all done on the Saturday, leaving the Sunday for me to relax for once. So, I didn't go to my usual Costa Coffee shop. I wanted to make sure that I didn't see the stranger again. I knew that if I did, the distraction would leave me in work deficit once more. I wasn't going to risk that.

I could have stayed at home. But being single, and on my own, I found it easier to work if I was surrounded by people and voices. Strange, I know, but it worked for me. I drove to a shopping centre and was about to set myself up in the small food hall when I saw him.

He was sitting alone at a table, scooping at a bowl of ice cream. I stopped dead, staring, but quickly recovered myself and turned around. In minutes I was back in my car, heading away, across town. Looking back, I should have gone home, instead I drew up in a garden centre car park and made my way inside.

The restaurant was full, and I had to queue for a coffee and a cake. Luckily, I stumbled upon a free table in a secluded area at the back, and it wasn't long before I immersed myself in my work.

"Do you mind if I sit here?"

The voice broke through my concentration. I looked up and there he was. My mouth fell open, and I just stared into his bright blue eyes.

"All the tables are full."

He gestured with his tray at the other tables. I couldn't take my gaze away from his face to check if what he was saying was true. I just stared.

He grinned at me, exposing white, even teeth. Taking my silence as assent, he placed his tray down and transferred the contents to the table.

"Sure," I croaked, as he lowered his tall frame into the chair opposite. He was wearing a plaid shirt with the sleeves rolled up, exposing muscled forearms covered in multicoloured tattoos.

"What are you up to?" he asked, nodding at my papers as he took a gulp of coffee.

Before I knew what I was doing, I blurted out that I was a massively over worked teacher, that I was single and had no life. He told me his name: Mike, and I told him everything about me. I couldn't help myself. I was like a teenager who'd met their first crush.

That was how it started. At the time, I didn't question anything about it. I didn't think to ask how come he was at the Garden Centre. I didn't think to ask if he'd been following me. Spoiler alert, he had. I know that now. I should have asked, but I was too enthralled with his presence. He was overwhelming. He was charming and funny and very, very masculine. I completely fell for him.

Inevitably, we ended up in bed. Again, now I can see how odd it was. I drove him to my flat and never thought to ask about his own car, and he never mentioned it. I know now that he didn't have one. He didn't need one.

The sex was beyond anything I had ever experienced. Even though I wasn't inexperienced and knew my way around a man's body, this was on a whole new level. He seemed to have an innate understanding of what I wanted, effortlessly moving his hands where I wanted or applying more pressure with no prompting from me. He knew exactly where to touch and how to please me. It was utterly mind-blowing.

The next few days were sheer bliss. I was head over heels in love. I couldn't help myself. He was totally intoxicating. I was completely in love and wanted to be with him every second of every day and night. Don't get me wrong, he never hurt me or attempted to manipulate me. He was always kind and considerate. He had a way of knowing just what to do or say to bring joy to my life.

Of course, it didn't last.

You might ask yourself how I knew he was a telepath. Well, apart from the fact that there was no other way of explaining how he knew everything, I once caught him talking to someone else. We were in bed, and I think he thought I was asleep. I was on my side, facing away from him; he was snuggled up behind me with his right arm draped over me. I could feel his warmth behind me as he whispered quietly, engaged in a one-way conversation with persons unknown. I just lay there with his quiet voice lulling me to sleep.

The next day, he was gone.

The devastation overwhelmed me, and I was inconsolable. I had already neglected my work and now it got worse. I didn't go in and didn't answer any emails or calls. I couldn't stop crying. My heart ached. I tried calling and texting him to no avail, and it was only then that I realised I knew nothing about him. I didn't know where he lived or where he worked. I couldn't find him. I went to the Costa Coffee shop and sat for hours, hoping he would walk in. I did the same at the Garden Centre. It was all a waste of time. He was gone.

It was then that I made my mistake. I went to the police.

Foolishly, I thought he might be injured or lying in a ditch somewhere. My stupid brain wanted it to be true. I wanted there to be a logical reason for his disappearance. I couldn't accept that he'd deliberately left me.

The Police were no help at all. 'I'm sorry, madam, you can't report a person as missing if you don't have a full name or address,' they said.

They asked lots more questions, and I got angry. That was my second mistake.

I guess, looking back, I shouldn't blame them. All they saw was a mad woman shouting, crying and shouting about a missing person she knew by first name only. I can see how ridiculous it must have looked; how mad I must have seemed. So, I can't blame them for calling the on-call doctor.

By then, I was beyond upset. I was raving, kicking and screaming. They put me in a cell and the doctor gave me a sedative to calm me down. It worked, but I was out of it. I had snapped. Something inside me broke and I couldn't function. I turned into a listless and useless shell of a person. I didn't eat or drink, I just lay on my bunk.

And now, two weeks later, here I am sitting and gazing through the window at the rainy sky.

"Hello Jane, how are you feeling today?" asked my friend as she sat next to me.

"I'm perfectly well," I replied.

"Good," she answered. "Do you think you are well enough to take a walk in the garden?"

I frown at her. Of course I am, there's nothing wrong with me. But I don't care about the garden.

"Have you found Mike?" I ask urgently.

She looks sad.

"Oh Jane," she sighs. "I've already explained that Mike doesn't exist. He isn't real. Your psychosis made him up."

I lunge forward and grip her hand hard.

"No!" I shout at her. "He's real, he's as real as you or I. I need to find him. Please help me!"

Her frown deepens, and I see her beckon behind her with her free hand.

"He's a telepath," I hiss at her, spittle flying from my lips. "He can read minds. He knows how to hide. I saw a documentary on TV about telekinesis and a secret society. He's one of them." I couldn't prevent my voice from getting louder. "I have to find him!"

My friend's expression changes to one of sympathy.

"Alright Jane," she says soothingly. "We'll see what we can do." Her eyes flick sideways and up. I turn just in time to see a man plunge a syringe into my upper arm.

"No!" I scream, but the drug takes effect quickly and I fall back into my chair. As my eyelids slowly close and I descend into blackness, I hear my friend talking.

"She's completely psychotic. She's fixated on this imaginary man she uses to explain her condition. Take her back to her cell. I can't see her ever recovering."

Trevor

Trevor wasn't the most successful or dynamic person in the world. He lived day to day, content with doing ordinary things that ordinary people did. He watched TV, played computer games, slept most of the day and worked most of the night.

He lived alone in a small bedsit on the high street. His marriage of three years had ended suddenly when he discovered his wife was having an affair. Then, eight months ago, he lost his job at a local school, where he was one of three caretakers. He had been dismissed for turning up drunk. With no other options, he had taken a job as a barman at the town's only nightclub.

Some might put these events down to Trevor making bad choices or just misfortune. But he didn't think about it like that. He lived for the here and now, and right now he was happy.

He was happy because, at the nightclub, he met Rosie.

Rosie had lustrous jet-black hair with an alluring, exotic complexion reflecting her Asian heritage. She had a slender, athletic figure he found incredibly attractive. She was like no other woman he had ever seen, and that she danced on stage every night didn't worry him in the slightest.

The fist slammed into his left cheek once more, his face exploding in pain as he fell to the ground. Even now, he couldn't stop thinking of Rosie. She was always uppermost in his mind. Right now, he wondered when he would drum up the courage to ask her out. They could grab a bite to eat somewhere, or catch a movie, or simply take a casual walk in the nearby park. She would laugh at his jokes and flash those lovely brown eyes at him from underneath her long eyelashes. They would share smiles, both knowing that the night would inevitably end with them making love at her place.

All he could think about was Rosie's radiant smile and laughing eyes. Then he hit the ground, the impact sending a jolt of pain through his wrist as he instinctively reached out to soften the impact.

"Keep away from my Rosie, or next time I'll kill you!" the gruff voice snarled from above him.

Pain flared in his ribs as his attacker left him with a parting kick.

He couldn't move, pain throbbing in his cheek, wrist and ribs as he gasped for air while the rain poured down, soaking through his clothes.

After a while, he found he could sit up to rest his back against the cold brick wall behind him. His clothes were completely soaked. His jeans were torn, most likely from the fall, and his left wrist throbbed with agony. Every breath brought a sharp jolt of pain in his chest, making him wonder if he had a broken rib. His watch was smashed, the hands frozen at two in the morning.

He sat there unable to think of anything besides his breathing and the pain, watching, without really seeing, a rat scuttling and sniffing around the collection of rubbish bins on the opposite side of the alleyway.

He had done nothing to warrant an attack, had he? He didn't think so. Of course, he hadn't known that Rosie had a boyfriend, although he wasn't surprised.

That evening had been the same as every other evening. He worked his shift behind the bar, serving customers all night, while keeping a lookout for Rosie to appear on stage. As soon as she did, he took his break and stood at the end of the bar, mesmerized by her routine, clapping and cheering with the rest of the audience as she removed her last item of clothing.

He smiled to himself at the memory, wincing at the pain in his cheek. Her boyfriend wouldn't last, he knew. She would discard him. Someone with her beauty and talent could have anyone. He wondered briefly if he should send her flowers, but then dismissed the idea. It was too soon. Maybe in another couple of weeks. Besides, he would have to wait for payday.

He was feeling recovered enough to get up to make his way back to his tiny bedsit when he heard footsteps.

Trevor's heart sank as he saw a dark figure approaching at the entrance of the alley. He knew he couldn't escape Rosie's violent boyfriend. Fear washed over him, bracing himself for another round of physical abuse; there was nothing he could do to stop it.

He watched with resignation as the figure slowly made its way towards him. Something seemed out of place, something not quite right. It wasn't the black coat and hood which made it impossible to see the face; it was something else. He couldn't quite grasp it, but he knew for certain that things were not as they should be.

Soon, the figure towered above, its head leaning down to study him. The shadows still concealing its face. Trevor gazed up at it in defeat. Then something caught his eye. He saw what was off about the figure. Despite the heavy downpour, it remained completely dry. It stood there, untouched by the rain, as if an invisible protective shield surrounded it and diverted the water away. The rain seemed to cascade around the figure, creating a curtain of water that spilled onto the ground below, splashing noisily on the tarmac.

For a full minute, the shadowy figure stood, statue still, looming over him, the rain bouncing and sliding down the transparent umbrella. Then it spoke.

"You're perfect."

To Trevor's surprise, a slightly raspy but distinctly feminine voice reached his ears. Despite the loud downpour of rain from the nearby roofs and gutters, he could still make out her undisguised, triumphant tone.

He watched, transfixed, as her hands reached up to throw back the hood and then gasped in shock.

Clear, green, almost luminous eyes stared down at him, framed by wild red hair. Freckles dotted her lightly tanned skin, giving her a youthful and vibrant appearance, and her full lips curled upwards in a radiant smile, making his heart skip a beat.

"I need you." She announced, her smile broadening, showing white, even teeth.

Trevor didn't know what to say. Entranced by her beauty and surprised at her statement, he just stared open-mouthed up at her, oblivious to the rain running from his balding pate, dripping onto his shoulders and running down his back.

All thoughts of his beloved Rosie left his mind, replaced by this flaming haired angel standing before him. What did she mean? How should he respond? Need him for what? Sex?

"Who are you?" he asked, wincing at the pain in his cheek which spasmed in time with his words.

She tilted her head to one side, a playful glint in her eyes as she licked her lips with a pink tongue. The quick flickering movement giving the impression of a playful cat, ready to pounce.

"You can call me," she paused, as if considering her next words, tilting her head to the other side. "Bee."

Trevor was in no doubt that Bee was not her real name. What sort of name was that, anyway? Short for Beatrice? Or just made up?

He cupped his injured cheek with his hand and pressed lightly to reduce the movement. "What do you want?" he asked, his voice slightly slurred.

She didn't reply. Instead, she slid off a pair of black leather gloves, her movements slow and deliberate, almost sensual. Trevor was mesmerised as she eased her fingers out, one by one, revealing perfectly manicured fingernails, each one painted in a different colour.

"You're injured," she pointed out, dropping her gloves. Trevor followed their motion as they hit the ground with a distinct splat, splashing in the rainwater.

His heart jumped when she abruptly extended her right hand towards him, her fingers splayed. He instinctively pulled his head back and hit it against the wall behind him with a dull thud. The sharp and sudden pain caused him to gasp and squeeze his eyes shut. Which meant that he didn't see the blue glow enveloping her outstretched hand in a gauntlet of light.

As if the sharp pain in his head wasn't enough, Trevor suddenly felt a jolt of electric current course through his body, causing his limbs to spasm uncontrollably. Fortunately, the jolt was short-lived and dissipated as quickly as it had come.

"Shit!" Trevor shouted, but then clamped his mouth tight shut as he realised that something had changed.

All his pain was gone.

His wrist, ribs and cheek no longer hurt. It was impossible. What had happened? He flexed his wrist carefully and then rubbed at his cheek. Nothing. Completely normal. A bright chuckle from above made him look up at the woman who called herself Bee.

"Come," she laughed at him, her eyes sparkling with mischief. "Follow me."

She turned away and walked back down the alley.

"Wait!" shouted Trevor. "What just happened? Who are you really? What's going on?"

Bee didn't stop walking.

"Follow me and find out," she called over her shoulder.

Trevor struggled to his feet. Rainwater soaked his clothes, and it dripped from his chin and dirty fingers. Muck smothered his jeans and shirt, sticking to his skin like glue, and he felt cold. Shivering, he stumbled after the mysterious woman, losing sight of her as she rounded a corner.

When he reached the corner, he stopped. Bee was nowhere to be seen. He frowned, casting his gaze back and forth, trying to locate her. Where had she gone? Had she got in a car and driven off? But then, she had asked him to follow. It made no sense. Why would she do that only to disappear?

Then he caught sight of her. Across the street, sitting in the window of a cafe, was a woman. Her fiery red hair gave her away. It was wild and full, just as he remembered it.

He noticed her watching him as he made his way across the quiet street. She held a cup delicately in both hands up to her mouth, her eyes locked on him over its rim.

Inside the cafe, it was warm and bright and completely empty apart from Bee and a waitress standing behind the serving counter. Trevor squelched his way over to Bee's table and sat opposite her. Water dripped from his clothes onto the floor, seat and table, quickly forming pools all around him. She continued to stare at him over the rim of her cup, her green eyes sparkling in the bright light.

The silence between them was broken by the waitress, who wordlessly placed a mug of steaming black coffee in front of him. Trevor looked up and watched as she walked away. A chink of china on china brought his attention back to Bee as she placed her cup in its saucer.

After wiping the dirt from his hands on his jeans, Trevor picked up the mug of coffee and took a sip, savouring the hot bitterness of the drink.

"Better?" Bee asked.

Trevor nodded and took another sip.

"Are you going to tell me what's going on?" he asked, placing his mug back on the table and wiping the dampness from his face with the back of his hand.

"It's simple," Bee responded, gracefully lifting her cup. Trevor watched her sipping what must have been a herbal tea, the liquid being very pale and watery. "I need you to get something for me." She flashed another of her dazzling smiles.

"I meant, how come my wrist and ribs no longer hurt? Did you do something? What did you do?"

"Oh, that." She fluttered her eyelashes at him while tapping a ring on a finger against her teacup. "It was nothing. Consider it a down payment." She took another sip from her cup.

Trevor frowned.

"Down payment for what?"

He watched as she returned her cup to its saucer. She leaned back in her seat and crossed her arms, her coat shifting, revealing a tantalising glimpse of red lace peeking out from underneath. She caught his gaze and narrowed her eyes, a sly smile playing on her lips.

"For doing what I want, of course," she answered.

"And that's getting something for you? What? Why can't you get it yourself? Why do you need me?" Asked Trevor, brushing the wet, long and thin strands of hair back from his face, slicking them over the top of his head.

A brief flash of irritation flickered across her angelic features, quickly replaced by the ever-present knowing smile. She turned away, surveying the interior of the cafe, allowing him a glimpse of her profile and the shimmering waterfall of hair cascading down her shoulders. He had seen no one like her. She reminded him of a movie star with her flawless beauty.

He followed her gaze towards the serving counter, where the waitress busied herself placing cups and mugs on the top of the espresso coffee machine. The gentle clinking of china on metal filling the space with familiar and soothing sounds. For a moment, he wondered why the waitress wasn't concerned at the mess he was making, the pools of dirty water still growing beneath his chair. Then Bee raised her teacup, gesturing with it towards the waitress, who nodded back, her expression serious.

Bee refocussed her attention on him.

"What would you like?" she asked.

It took a few seconds for Trevor to realise that she wasn't talking about coffee or cake, but he wasn't sure what she was asking.

"What do you mean?"

She looked a little frustrated.

"In payment," she explained.

Trevor picked up his mug and took a few gulps. What was going on? What did she mean about getting something for her? What could it be? He suddenly had a thought. Maybe it was dangerous? Maybe she wanted him to risk his life for her?

"A lot of money," he replied automatically.

Her smile widened.

"No, that's not it," she told him.

"Huh?"

"That's not what you want," she explained patiently.

Trevor put down his mug, thumping it onto the table in anger.

"Try again," Bee told him.

Trevor opened his mouth to object but stopped when the waitress reappeared with another cup and saucer, setting them down in front of Bee. The two women shared a knowing look, clearly communicating something without saying a word.

He narrowed his eyes and started to think that this whole situation he found himself in was some kind of setup. He hadn't thought about it before, but now he thought more clearly. The waitress and Bee obviously knew each other. And Bee, so far, had told him nothing. She spoke in riddles and had explained nothing. And how come she was dry? He was completely drenched, yet she sat across from him, looking perfect. He remembered that invisible curtain that seemed to protect her from the rain. And how come his injuries were healed? None of what was happening made any sense, and he'd had enough. He felt the anger build in him, his face flushing.

He stood quickly, scraping his chair backwards, the noise shattering the silence of the cafe.

"I've had enough of this bullshit!" he exclaimed. "I don't care what you want or who you are. You can find some other schmuck to bamboozle with your crap!"

He turned, fully intending to exit the cafe and make his way to his bedsit. He needed to get out of these wet clothes before he caught a cold or the flu.

"Stop."

Her voice was soft, barely above a whisper, yet it carried a weight and power that stopped him in his tracks. It was not a command, but a suggestion that somehow held more force than a yell could. The sound of her words echoed through his mind. He discovered he couldn't move; his muscles refused to obey him, rendering him frozen like a statue.

"Sit."

Once more, her voice was a gentle suggestion rather than a command, but its power was undeniable. Before he knew what was happening, he had turned back and resumed his seat at the table.

With her arms tightly crossed and a look of disdain etched across her face, the waitress rigidly stood behind Bee, who remained seated at the table. Bee's smile was gone, replaced by a stone-cold expression. Her eyes flashed with fierce determination and her eyebrows furrowed in annoyance.

"I'm not ready for you to leave," she explained in an icy voice that sent shivers down his spine. "You will answer my question and you will answer it truthfully."

She sat back, picking up her teacup once more, bringing it up to her mouth slowly.

"What do you want?"

For the second time that night, Trevor felt fear grow from the pit of his stomach, invading his mind, turning it to treacle and sending ice flowing in his veins. Who was this woman? One thing was obvious: she was no ordinary woman. His thoughts crumbled into an incoherent jumble of disjointed words that made no sense. But one word surfaced, and he found himself saying it again and again in his head: Witch!

As he struggled to regain his senses, he watched as Bee continued sipping at her tea, her elbows tucked in to her body, waiting for him to reply.

At first, he wasn't sure what to say. If not money, then what? A new job? Or a car? What sort of thing was she expecting him to say? His thoughts went round and round in circles as he thought desperately.

One thing was sure, he had underestimated this woman. Somehow, she could make him do things; how, he didn't know.

Suddenly, he had it. He knew what he wanted.

"Rosie," he whispered, feeling ashamed.

Bee nodded sagely.

"That's the one," she answered, placing her cup back in its saucer. Unfolding her arms, the waitress behind her walked away, as if she too was satisfied with his answer. She soon arrived back at the serving counter, where she resumed placing and rearranging coffee mugs and cups. Trevor wondered if she worked here. A moment ago, it looked as though the two women knew each other, maybe even worked together. Now, he wasn't so sure. How come she was working behind the counter? What was going on?

"If you do something for me, I promise you will have your Rosie," Bee continued. "Does that sound good to you?"

Trevor grimaced, a frown on his face.

"You can't promise me that," he said dismissively. "No one can."

Bee smiled broadly, revealing her perfect teeth.

"No ordinary person, I grant you," she answered. "But, as I am sure that you have realised by now, I'm no ordinary woman. I assure you; I can give you what you want."

A sound of disbelief escaped Trevor's lips, then he clamped his mouth shut. Clearly, she meant what she said. He watched as she reached beneath her coat with delicate fingers to retrieve a cigarette packet and lighter. As she withdrew her hand, the fabric of her coat parted, teasingly revealing more of the lacy red garment underneath and the curves of her ample bosom.

A small snicker escaped her lips when she noticed his gaze.

"Do you believe me?" she asked, extracting a cigarette from the packet.

With an effort, Trevor tore his eyes from her chest.

"No."

Bee busied herself putting the cigarette in her mouth and lighting it. She inhaled deeply and blew out smoke from the side of her mouth.

"You should," she replied. "How are your injuries?" She gestured to his body with her cigarette hand.

Instinctively, Trevor put a hand to his ribs.

"How do you think that happened?" she asked, putting the cigarette to her mouth.

"You said that you did it, but that's obviously crap," Trevor replied.

Her smile reached deep into his soul, causing his heart to flutter. He couldn't deny her beauty; it was natural and exuded a sensuality that few women had. Just moments ago, he had been afraid of her, maybe even under her control - though he couldn't be certain of that. But now, he found himself drawn to her in a way that reminded him of how he felt when he saw his beloved Rosie strutting her stuff on the stage.

"You have another explanation?" She paused, breathing out smoke. "No, of course you don't. I did it. I healed you. You need to be in good condition. I can't have you limping into the bank."

Trevor was silent. What could he say? She was talking nonsense, or she was telling the truth. Obviously, it was nonsense. It couldn't possibly be true. But he couldn't explain how his injuries were gone. Then he caught something she had just said.

"Did you say bank?"

She took another pull from her cigarette and gestured to the window. Trevor followed her gaze. On the opposite side of the road, amid the shops, there was a bank. A sign with its logo lit up yellow although at this time of night it was closed.

Understanding came to him. She wanted him to rob the bank across the street.

"You've got to be joking!" he exclaimed, half laughing at her. "There's no way I'm holding up a bank, no matter what you promise!"

If anything, Bee's smile grew wider.

"Who said anything about holding it up? All you need to do is retrieve the contents of a deposit box for me."

Trevor was taken-a-back. Her response was not what he expected. He frowned once more. Could the evening get any stranger?

"Hold on," he objected. "You want me to enter that bank across the street, unlock a deposit box and bring the contents to you? Is that what you're asking?"

Bee nodded, puffing on the last of her cigarette and then stubbing it out in her now empty teacup.

"That's exactly what I need you to do."

"Why can't you do it yourself? You don't need me. Why all the cloak and dagger stuff?" He waved a damp arm, gesturing to the empty cafe.

"It's complicated," replied Bee, taking out another cigarette from the packet. "Let's just say I can't and leave at that, shall we?"

Trevor was confused. He'd been confused ever since meeting her, so this was nothing new. But now something clicked in his mind. If that was all she wanted, then maybe he could get something more out of this bizarre situation. He didn't believe what she had said about Rosie for one minute, but maybe he could get more. What if he asked for cash as well? Would she agree? She looked wealthy, so surely, she could afford a few thousand?

"Is it safe?" he asked. "I mean, it's all perfectly legal and I won't get arrested or something?"

Bee inhaled from her cigarette.

"It's perfectly safe for you. All you do is go in, get the contents and then bring it to me."

Trevor thought about it some more. It sounded too easy.

"What's in the box?"

"Inside the deposit box, there's a small black bag. That's what I need."

He picked up his coffee mug and took a sip of the by now, lukewarm liquid as he considered his options. He could walk out, but he'd already tried that. It hadn't gone well. Whomever this Bee was, she had some way of controlling him. Or he could accept her proposal. It sounded easy, too easy. There must be a catch. But what was it?

"I'll do it if you throw in ten thousand," he stated resolutely, placing his coffee mug back on the table.

Bee flicked ash from her cigarette onto the floor.

"The deal is you get Rosie, nothing more."

She brushed at small particles of ash that had landed on her knee.

"You should know, as I hope you've realised, that you have no choice. I'm not asking you to agree, I'm giving you instructions. There is no negotiation here. You will do what I ask. I'm being kind by offering you a payment. I don't have to. You should be grateful."

Trevor couldn't help himself.

"Grateful!" he spat.

Bee nodded slowly, her movements slow and deliberate. She reached inside her coat and pulled out a key from beneath the red lace.

Placing it on the table in front of him, she explained, "This is the key to the deposit box."

Trevor automatically reached over and grabbed the key. It felt warm to the touch, making him think it had been tucked against her skin.

"This afternoon at one thirty pm, you will enter the bank over there." She nodded towards the window. "You will ask to access deposit box eight four three nine. You will then open the box and remove the small black bag. You will leave the bank with the bag in your pocket, and you will cross the street to enter this cafe. I will be sitting here at this table. There will be no one else here apart from myself and Lena." She nodded towards the serving counter and inhaled from her cigarette once more. "You will hand over the bag to me and then you will leave. You will never see me again. In the evening, you will go to work as usual, and Rosie will be yours."

She flicked the cigarette into her cup and stood, using her hands to smooth out her long, black coat before pulling up the hood over her untamed red hair.

"There's nothing more to be said. I'll see you this afternoon."

He watched the waitress join her and the two of them exited the cafe hand in hand, leaving him alone. They didn't ask him to leave and didn't even try to lock up.

He sat, trying to make sense of what had just happened. Was she that naïve to think he would do as she asked? Because there was no way he was going to do it. Why should he? She had promised the impossible. Did she even know who Rosie was, or was it just a ploy to manipulate him? Very likely, he thought to himself.

It all felt like a surreal dream. It was all so strange and bizarre, as if it hadn't really happened. But he couldn't deny that it had - he had met an enigmatic and stunning woman named Bee. She had given him a key, which he still held in his hand. As he gazed at it lying in his palm, he couldn't deny her existence - she was real, and the key was solid proof of that.

He closed his fist around the key and squeezed, feeling the sharp edges bite into his skin. What should he do? Well, first things first, he needed to get out of these wet clothes. He would definitely not be going to the bank in the afternoon. As usual, he would sleep in and then watch TV until his shift at the bar started. He would watch Rosie perform on the stage and he would be happy. Standing quickly, he left the cafe, walking into the night.

When he arrived at the tiny room he called home, he stripped off his wet clothes. A hot shower in the communal bathroom warmed him up, and he felt clean again. Later, he crawled into his narrow bed and drifted off to sleep. Images of two women dancing on a stage: one with fiery red hair, while the other had long, dark locks, filled his dreams.

―――

The next day at one thirty pm, Trevor found himself standing outside the bank. He wasn't sure how it had happened. He had eaten breakfast, played some computer games and then left his bedsit, intending to buy some groceries. Instead, he was outside the bank.

He couldn't remember making his way here. In fact, the last thing he recalled was closing the door to his tiny room. He had no memory of walking through the town, and certainly no memory of going to a grocery store. Looking down, he saw that the bag he carried was empty.

With a slight turn of his head, he gazed across the bustling street to the cafe opposite. And there she was, just as he had expected, sitting at the same table. Her fiery red locks were impossible to miss. They stood out like a flaming beacon in the sea of people passing by.

A feeling of uneasiness built in his stomach. He had made a conscious decision not to do this, yet somehow, he found himself here, against his better judgment. Was it her doing? How? How had she swayed him? Or was it simply his own desire to please her, blinded by her beauty? He didn't have an answer.

His hand automatically went to his jeans pocket, where he felt the familiar outline of the key. He hesitated, unsure of what to do next. Looking around, he saw the bustle of everyday life; people walking, cars and bikes passing by. It was a typical day, no different from any other. Then his gaze locked with hers. She was watching him keenly, the ever-present teacup in her hand, her green eyes obvious, even from this distance.

He entered the bank.

Inside, it was easy to request access to the deposit box room. There, a wall greeted him, filled with hundreds of small doors, each with a keyhole and a number neatly engraved next to it.

He quickly located number eight four three nine, inserted the key, and removed the box. Placing it on a table, he opened it, and sure enough, it contained a small black cloth bag. He gazed at it for some time, wondering if he was doing the right thing. Why couldn't Bee do this? Why did she need him to do it? There were the usual security guards, but they didn't question his authority, just eyed him from a distance. He had followed the bank official to the deposit box room. Nothing seemed out of the ordinary. Sure, the official was wearing a lot of jewellery, but that wasn't uncommon in today's society. Each finger adorned with a shiny gold ring and tiny golden chains connecting them didn't raise any red flags, at least not beyond a cursory glance.

He was back to the fundamental question: why did Bee need him to retrieve this bag? He would probably never know. With a quick movement, he extracted the bag and placed it into his jeans pocket. He then replaced the box and relocked its door.

No one challenged him as he left the bank. He waited for a gap in the traffic and crossed the road, acutely aware that Bee was watching his every move. When he entered the cafe, it was exactly the same as last night. There were no customers, just the waitress behind the serving counter and Bee sat waiting at the same table, just as she said she would be.

As he approached her table, Bee stood, obvious eagerness in her manner and expression. Holding out her hand, she didn't say a word as he passed her the small black bag.

An expression of triumph spread across her face, lighting up every feature as she closed her delicate fingers around the bag. She pressed it against her chest and gently closed her eyes, a contented sigh escaping from between her lips. Whatever was in the bag, it was clearly precious to her.

"What is it?" he asked, curiosity getting the better of him.

She opened her eyes, their luminescence fixed on him.

"Power," she responded before walking past him towards the exit.

Trevor turned and watched her leave, the waitress following behind. Once again, he was alone in the cafe, and once again he wondered if he had done the right thing.

He looked at his watch. He had two hours before his shift started.

―――

The audience erupted into a frenzy of cheers as Rosie confidently strutted across the stage, wearing only black high heels. Trevor, as always, had claimed his spot at the end of the bar, giving him an unobstructed view of her captivating performance. He joined in with the rest of the crowd, clapping and cheering as she reached the end of her set, and she walked off the stage.

He was nearing the end of his break and was about to resume serving behind the bar when a light tap on his shoulder made him spin around. He couldn't believe his eyes. It was Rosie. She had draped herself in a sheer, airy wrap that left concealed very little.

Her smile caused his heart to leap, and then she spoke the words that he had always imagined she would one day.

"Buy me a drink?"

From that moment on, the night transformed into the most incredible experience of his life. They shared playful banter at the bar, with her giggling at his jokes and batting her eyelashes seductively. At some point, she excused herself and returned wearing a tight and alluring little black dress. She reclaimed her spot at the bar, patiently waiting for him to finish his shift.

Later, they walked arm in arm to her flat. Trevor could hardly contain himself. Just as Bee had promised, he was with Rosie. Somehow Bee had done it. She had said that he would have Rosie and here she was, clinging onto his arm, laughing and smiling seductively up at him. He was so happy. He had done the right thing after all.

He was so preoccupied that he didn't hear the footsteps behind him until it was too late.

Pain flared as a blow in his lower back thrust him forward.

"I already told you. You get with my Rosie again, I'll kill you!" the gruff voice shouted.

Rosie's scream echoed in his ears as he stumbled to land on his knees. The pain was overwhelming, causing his vision to blur. He struggled to catch his breath and instinctively reached around to feel the source of the agony on his back. When he brought his hand back, he saw it was covered in blood. He stared at it, disbelieving. A wave of nausea and weakness washed over him. The ground rushed up at him and he found himself lying on his side. From his prone position, he saw a powerfully built man dragging a kicking and screaming Rosie along the pavement, the two of them fading away into the distance.

The world around him dimmed as his vision slowly faded. His body grew stiff, the warmth draining away as his lifeblood seeped around him. With his thoughts slowing to a sluggish pace, he could feel himself succumbing to the frigid chill that enveloped him. His fingers grew numb, and his breath came out in quick gasps. He knew with certainty that he was dying.

His final thoughts were of Bee. She had been telling the truth the whole time. For a brief few hours, he had been happy with his Rosie and it was thanks to Bee. He wished he could see her one last time to thank her, but that wasn't going to happen. Briefly, he worried about Rosie and hoped that she would be okay. But he knew she would be fine. A woman with Rosie's looks and talents could have anyone she wanted.

The Witch

Present Day

Carl Rodriguez ran up the stairs in a fruitless attempt to catch his children, who were already charging towards their bedroom. As usual, the anticipation of a bedtime story had infused them with boundless energy and excitement.

Breathing heavily, he burst into their bedroom to find both Phoebe and David tucked up in bed, their eager faces alight with smiles and anticipation.

"What'll it be tonight?" he asked, smiling back at them and walking over to the large bookshelf. "Swallows and Amazons, or Harry Potter?"

"Tell us about the witch!" exclaimed Phoebe, her tiny voice full of joy.

"Yeah, dad, tell us about when you met the witch," said David, agreeing with his twin sister.

Carl turned and looked down at them, their smiling faces full of excitement and eagerness.

"You've heard that story a million times already. Surely you don't want me to tell it again?" he complained.

The twins shrieked back at him.

"Yes, we do! We love it!"

Carl sighed exaggeratedly.

"Alright. Scoot up then."

Phoebe and David moved up, making space for him to join them in the large double bed.

"Are you ready?" he asked once he had made himself comfortable.

Two tiny faces looked at him with love and adoration as they waited.

"Very well. It happened eight years ago in December. I was driving back home after a late night at work."

Carl knew he couldn't tell his children exactly what had happened that night. They weren't old enough to understand, so he adapted his story to make it child friendly.

Eight Years Ago

It was one of those dirty nights that made driving difficult. It was drizzling, the rain a fine mist that even his headlights on full beam couldn't penetrate. And then, when an approaching car appeared, forcing him to dip his lights, he could see even less. As a result, Carl was not making good time. The hedges and trees flashed by as he sped along as fast as he could, given the conditions, which was not as quick as he would like. He was going to miss his date with Monica.

He grunted in frustration as, yet another car appeared in the distance, forcing him to dip his lights and slow slightly to compensate for his lack of vision. Concentrating hard and trying to see through the darkness caused a headache to form across his brow, which wasn't helping.

As soon as the car heading towards him passed on the opposite side of the road, he flicked his lights to main beam and sped up, his speedometer approaching the speed limit of sixty miles an hour. For the next ten minutes, the road was empty, enabling to make good progress towards his destination.

And then something strange and unexpected interrupted his journey.

A bright blue light lit up the sky and landscape ahead. For a full two seconds, the intense brightness banished the night, casting long shadows of trees and buildings across the wet road and nearby fields.

The intensity combined by its sudden appearance caught Carl by surprise, its brightness causing him to close his eyes tight, pain flaring behind his eyelids. Unable to open his eyes to view the road, he slammed on the brakes; the tyres squealing as he the car slid to a halt.

His heart racing and adrenaline coursing through his veins, Carl opened his eyes to find he had come to a halt on the wrong side of the road. He'd been lucky that there were no oncoming vehicles. A head on crash would have been serious. Quickly, he drove the car to the right side of the road and pulled over, turning on his hazard lights.

Putting the car into neutral, he let go of the steering wheel and removed his feet from the pedals. Taking in a deep breath, he let it out slowly while running his hands through his hair and across his face. That had been close!

He flicked on the interior light and gazed at himself in the rear-view mirror, seeing his deep blue eyes staring back at him, the pupils wide. He took a moment to study himself, the slightly receding hairline, the long black beard, and the thick eyebrows and wondered if Monica would find him attractive. But then dismissed the thought as quickly as it came. The point was academic. He was already twenty minutes late for his blind date. There was no way she would be there by the time he arrived.

Present Day

"What was the light, dad?" asked David.

He was the elder twin by five minutes, his shock of blond hair falling across his forehead, obscuring his dark brown eyes.

"I never found out," answered Carl.

"Did you ask the witch?" asked Phoebe.

Just like her sibling, she, too, had blonde hair. However, unlike David, hers cascaded down her back and framed her face beautifully. As she gazed up at him, with her bright blue eyes and adorable pug nose wrinkling slightly. She was going to be a real beauty, just like her mother.

"I did later," nodded Carl, smiling down at his daughter. "But I didn't understand what she said."

"How come dad?" asked David. "Did she speak an alien language?"

Carl laughed.

"No, no. She used big technical words that I didn't understand." He ruffled his son's hair. "You know I'm not very good with technical things."

David grinned.

"Yep, Phoebe had to show you how to do a series link on the Sky box yesterday!"

"Yeah, well, I don't know why things need to be so complicated," answered Carl defensively.

"Never mind, dad," said Phoebe. "We still love you. You can't help it if you're useless!"

Carl put his arm around his two children and squeezed them to him.

"Thanks," he said dryly. "You two are the cheekiest kids I know! It's a good job you're mine, otherwise I might send you back!"

"Awe dad," whined David. "Tell us what happened next."

Eight Years Ago

It took a couple of minutes for Carl to recover. The flash had long gone and hadn't been repeated. He wondered if it had been an explosion, maybe from a power plant or a factory or maybe even from a plane crash. But he hadn't heard a loud bang. There had been only the flash. It could have been a weather phenomenon, a lightning flash. It was raining, after all.

He reached over, turned on the radio, and selected a news channel, certain that if there had been an explosion or plane crash, the news would have reported it. But after listening for a couple of minutes, there was no mention of anything that could have caused the flash.

Carl shrugged and switched off the radio. He put the car into gear and resumed his journey. Whatever the flash was, it was probably nothing. It couldn't have been an explosion or a crash, so it was most likely sheet lightning. Although, as he drove, he suddenly realised that there had been no accompanying boom of thunder.

By now, he realised he would be over an hour late for his date with Monica. There was no point in turning up; she would be long gone. He found it surprising that she hadn't called him, but he knew she would eventually, and he would have to come up with some excuse. Because the truth was, he didn't want to meet her. He was tired. It had been a long day and truth be told; he wasn't interested in a relationship right now.

Present Day

"Was Monica nice, dad?" asked Phoebe.

"Who cares?" complained David.

"Be nice, David," Carl gently chided. "I don't know Pheebs, I never met her. But I bet she was a really nice person."

"But you didn't want to meet her?" asked Phoebe.

"Not really. I was tired."

"It's a good job you didn't," David stated matter-of-factly. "Or you wouldn't have met the witch."

Carl nodded.

"That's right, I wouldn't have met the witch." He squeezed them once more.

"What happened next?" asked David.

Eight Years Ago

It wasn't long before Carl turned off the main carriageway and drove onto a winding B road surrounded on both sides by tall trees. He had decided. He had no intention of meeting Monica. Tomorrow, he would have to face the music. Right now, he wanted to get home. His bed was calling, and his headache was getting worse.

If anything, the night seemed even darker, the trees arching over the road on both sides. But at least he could leave his lights on full beam, there being no other traffic. The bright headlights and the trees cast strange moving shadows as he rounded bend after bend.

After another fifteen minutes, he wasn't far from the small village that he called home when it happened again.

The intense blue light flashed from somewhere ahead, blinding him, causing him to cry out in pain and throw up an arm across his eyes. Once again, he slammed on the brakes, but this time, he was not so lucky. He felt the car bounce as it left the road and then a shriek of branches scraping across metal as the car ploughed into low-growing trees and bushes.

As the car slid to a stop, he pried his eyes open. Through the blurred lights lingering on his retinas, he let out a breath of relief as he realised, he had narrowly avoided colliding with a tree.

He sat, waiting for the afterimages to go and his breathing to slow. When he could eventually see properly, he got out of the car to survey the damage. Dismayed, he saw that the car's front wheels were buried in grassy mud. The rain had soaked the ground, making it sticky and soft. In a way that was good - it had slowed the car enough to prevent him from hitting a massive, old oak tree.

He cursed to himself. There was no way he was going to drive out of this. There would be no traction in the mud and while his headlights lit up the gigantic oak in front of the car, they didn't help light up the road behind. He couldn't see what else he had run over. There could be rocks or fallen trees, creating more obstacles to returning to the road. No. He wasn't getting out of here without a tow truck.

His shoulders slumped when he realised, he had no torch, coat, or umbrella. Walking the last couple of miles to the village would be out of the question. He leaned back into the car to retrieve his phone.

"Fuck!" he shouted when he saw he had no signal.

Present Day

"Were you angry, dad?" asked David.

"You could say that," answered Carl.

"I bet you used some naughty words," Phoebe stated, a serious expression on her face.

"I might have," grinned Carl.

"How close were you to that old tree?" asked David. "I bet it would have been a big crash if you'd hit it!"

"Very close, and yes, I was lucky to miss it."

"Dad, can I have a drink of hot chocolate?" Phoebe.

Carl raised his eyebrows.

"It's bedtime. You're supposed to be going to sleep."

"Aww, please?" her little face looked up at him, love in her eyes, her expression hopeful.

Carl sighed.

"Tell you what, I'll ask mum to bring up two hot chocolates after the story."

"Yay!" there were squeals of delight from each twin.

"But after your hot chocolate, it's bedtime. Okay?"

Two blonde heads nodded together.

"What happened next?"

Eight Years Ago

Although he hadn't crashed, there was no way he was going to get out of all that mud. Standing in the centre of the road, he looked both ways, but saw no other cars approaching that he could flag down. He focussed his attention on the phone signal indicator as he walked a little up the road. He was out of luck. There was still no signal.

He debated what to do. He was getting wet from the fine rain, and he would need a torch if he wanted to walk down the road.

Trouble was, he didn't have one. He could use the torch facility on his phone, but it was nowhere near as good as a proper torch. He didn't think that he had much choice.

Sighing, he made his way back to the car, switched off the engine and locked it. Then he walked down the road towards the village, using his phone to light the way.

It didn't take long for him to get thoroughly wet and miserable. He'd walked about a mile and still had no signal. The going was slow because of the limited amount of light available, and now he was worrying about the rain affecting his phone. It was soaked. He would be stranded in the dark if his phone stopped working.

He rounded a sharp bend and stopped in his tracks. There was something in the road. It was a body.

Present Day

Even though the twins knew this story well, they'd heard it many times before, they still asked questions.

"Was it dead?" asked David.

"Of course not, silly," replied Phoebe. "We know who it is."

"Yeah," replied David. "But it would have been cool if someone had died in the middle of the road."

"Ew, that's sick!" complained Phoebe.

"Calm down, you two," said Carl. "Do you want me to tell the story or not?"

"Yes!" the two of them chorused.

Eight Years Ago

Carl ran over to the body and knelt beside it. He hesitated. If someone had been hit by a car, they might have internal injuries and moving them could make things worse. But maybe he should find out if they were still alive first. He leant over to view the face and was surprised to see that it was a woman. Her pale, almost white, face was covered in grime and her eyes were closed. Her hair was short, dirty, wet and plastered to her neck and cheeks. She was wearing a dark long-sleeved top and trousers with a pair of black lace-up boots.

It took just seconds to take all this in. Then he leant close to her face and turned his ear towards her mouth. He could feel her breath on his cheek and hear her breathing softly. She was alive.

He sat back and wondered what he should do. He was no doctor, but he knew she could be seriously injured. Checking his phone, he was annoyed to see that he still had no signal. He debated picking her up and carrying her back to his car. Then she would be out of the rain. But would that make any of her injuries worse? And besides, could he carry her that far? He doubted it. How much further to the village? Probably another five miles. He could go get help and then come back, but how long would that take? She might die while he was gone.

He stood and looked down the road, first one way, then the other. No sign of any other cars. No sign of help.

"Help me up," commanded a female voice from behind him.

He whirled to find the woman attempting to stand. She was clutching her left arm and clearly in pain. He hurried over and grasped her right arm, trying to support her as she struggled to get up on her feet.

"Are you sure you should be moving around?" he asked with concern. "You might make things worse."

She gripped his arm with surprising strength, staring up at him, her blue eyes locking with his. They remained that way for a full ten seconds. Then she broke the spell.

"You'll do," she said, surveying her surroundings.

"I'll do?" he asked, feeling a little insulted.

"Do you have a vehicle?"

"Well, yes, but it's stuck in mud on the verge. I was walking for help when I found you."

"That's no problem," she replied, walking down the road back the way he had come. He noticed straight away that she had pronounced limp.

"Wait!" he called after her, hurrying after her. He caught up and slipped his arm around her waist for support. She flashed a sharp look before leaning into him, letting him assist her. He used his phone to light the road while she hobbled beside him. "The car is stuck. There's no point going back."

"I'll sort it," she replied mysteriously.

"You're hurt," Carl pointed out, changing tack. She was clearly determined. "You shouldn't be walking. You need to rest."

"No rest," she replied. "It's just a broken collarbone and a twisted ankle. I'll fix them when I can tap into the energy field."

Her determination puzzled Carl, as well as some of the things that she said. He briefly wondered if she had a head injury, but looking closely, he saw no signs of blood in her hair. As they walked, he caught a mix of scents emanating from her: a curious blend of sweat, dirt, and perfume that he found oddly captivating.

"What do you mean?" he asked.

"No time," she answered. "Have you seen anything?"

"Huh?"

She stopped and turned to look up at him.

"Have you seen anything unusual?" Her eyes were intense, her expression serious.

Present Day

"She's the witch, isn't she, dad?" asked David.

Carl nodded.

"Well, I didn't know it at the time, but yes, she's the witch."

"Did you like her?" asked Phoebe.

Carl shuffled uncomfortably.

"Well, not at first," he replied.

"I bet you were really surprised when she got up," David said matter-of-factly.

"I was. For a moment, I thought she might be dead. Fortunately, she was okay."

"She still had a twisted ankle and a broken arm," pointed out Phoebe.

"Broken collarbone," corrected Carl.

"Whatever," Phoebe dismissed. "What's this energy thing she was talking about?"

"I didn't know, and I guess I should have asked her, but I was about to find out."

"Yeah, Pheebs, let dad tell the story!" said David.

"I'm not the only one talking," pointed out Phoebe, her little mouth in a pout.

Carl raised a hand in a stop gesture.

"That's enough, you two. Do you want me to keep going?"

Two voices chorused as one: "Yes!"

Eight Years Ago

"Do you mean the flash?" asked Carl.

"That was just me entering your world. Have you seen anything else?"

By now, Carl was thinking that she sure that she had a head injury. She was talking nonsense.

"Did you arrive twice?" he chuckled.

She paused her limping walk and gazed up at him. She was a head shorter than him, with a stylish bob haircut and a straight fringe. Her blue eyes bore into his, framed by small freckles on her pale cheeks, a serious expression on her face. The misty rain had coated her eyebrows and upper lip with a fine sheen of moisture.

"What do you mean, twice?" she asked in a whisper.

He thought he detected a slight hint of fear in her voice.

"Well, there were two flashes," Carl started to explain but was cut off by the woman.

"We need to get moving!" She pulled him along, limping once more.

Carl resisted and pulled her back.

"Look, what's going on here?" he asked. "Are you sure you haven't got a head injury, because what you're saying makes no sense. I told you already, the car is stuck, there's no point going back to it. We'd be better off walking to the village."

A flicker of annoyance crossed her face, which was quickly replaced by resignation.

"I don't have a head injury," she replied. "Look," she hesitated, looked around and then faced him. "I know that this seems a bit," she hesitated once again. "Strange. I need you to believe me when I tell you we're in danger right now. I'm sorry you got dragged into this, but it's too late now. We need to get to your vehicle and get out of here."

"Well, you're right about one thing," Carl replied. "It's a bit strange. It's the middle of the night and I'm soaking wet. My car is stuck in the mud and a strange woman is talking about danger. Look, I want to help, but this isn't the way."

She was silent for a while, her gaze searching his face as if deciding what to do or say. Then she gently pulled away from his supporting arm.

"Alec, send a Spinker, a Koolu and a Recharge unit."

She spoke without breaking eye contact with him. He frowned in concern. It was obvious now that she had a head injury, and that it must be very serious if she could no longer form coherent sentences.

"I was going to wait until we got to your vehicle," she continued. "But as time is of the essence and you're going to take some convincing." She broke off and smiled up at him. "You seem like a decent bloke. I'm sorry for what you are about to go through." She held out her hand. "I'm Lena."

Carl automatically took her hand in his.

"Carl," he answered. "What do you mean, what I'm about to go through?"

She gazed up at him, a mixture of sadness and mischief on her face.

"Nice to meet you, Carl. You'll find out soon."

As if to confirm what she said, there was a snapping sound and three boxes appeared out of nowhere to thump onto the tarmac. Carl jumped, releasing Lena's hand.

"What the hell!" he exclaimed in shock.

"Don't panic," Lena told him. "Alec sent me the stuff I asked for. See that box there?" She indicated one of the three boxes; a squat silver box that was the smallest of the three. "Could you open it for me and pass me the contents?" She looked expectantly at him. "I can't bend down on this ankle and with this arm." She explained.

Carl did a double take.

"Who the hell is Alec? And where the fuck did these boxes come from?"

"I'll explain in a minute. Please pass me the contents of that small box."

Carl hesitated; his mind full of questions. Should he follow her instructions? What was inside the box? Where did they come from? And who exactly was this Alec person? The questions swirled endlessly in his head, making it hard to focus on just one.

"When you're ready," Lena's voice startled him back to the present and the rainy night.

Bending down, he unclasped the two spring-loaded catches on the smaller of the silver boxes. He lifted the lid to reveal a small black box, snugly cradled and cushioned in foam.

"Is this what you want?" he asked, lifting out the small black box.

Lena limped towards him.

"Give it to me!" she snapped, reaching out her hand and snatching from him.

Carl watched as she struggled to open it with only her right hand, her left still cradled to her body. It wasn't long before she gave an exasperated sigh.

"Here," she handed the box back. "Hold it."

Carl did as requested. While she manipulated something on its side. A flap opened, and she quickly pushed her hand inside. He yelped when he felt the box vibrate in his hand.

"Don't drop it!" she hissed at him.

He couldn't tear his eyes away as the box hummed gently, emitting a soft pink glow that flashed up Lena's arm to engulf her head. She tilted her head back and shut her eyes while Carl gasped in amazement. What was she doing? Her expression contorted as if she were experiencing pain. He had witnessed nothing like this before. What was happening? What was the box doing to her?

Then, as quickly as it had come, the glow disappeared, the humming and vibration stopped.

When he raised his eyes from the box to Lena, he was shocked to see that she had changed.

Present Day

"What was the witch doing?" asked David.

"Recharging, silly," answered Phoebe. "She needed to get her powers back."

"But how come she lost her powers in the first place?" asked David.

"Dad? Isn't Lena mum's name?" asked Phoebe.

"It is," answered Carl.

"Did she use her powers to kill zombies?" continued David, not to be swayed by his line of questioning.

"No David, she didn't kill any zombies," explained Carl. "And yes, Phoebe is right. She was recharging, she told me later."

Phoebe nodded. "I was right," she smiled smugly to herself.

"Only cos we've heard the story before," complained David.

"Now come on, you two. No fighting or it's straight to bed and no story."

"Sorry dad," said David.

"Sorry, dad," echoed Phoebe.

Eight Years Ago

Lena stood taller, no longer cradling her left arm, and her eyes were bright with a newfound sparkle. Even her cheeks had more colour. There was an energy about her, making her seem more vibrant and livelier.

Before he could ask her, what had caused the change, she stooped, picked up one of the two remaining boxes and set off, running along the dark road, her big boots thumping and splashing on the wet tarmac.

"Bring the Spinker," she called over her shoulder.

Carl watched her, dumbfounded. She was running. He couldn't understand it. A few minutes ago, she could hardly walk and now she was running. How was that possible? For a few seconds, he considered leaving her and resuming his walk to the village. It was all too much for him to comprehend, and all too strange. Whatever was going on here, it felt wrong. Either that or he was dreaming. He had an odd sense of foreboding. That if he followed her, he would be lost in her world and his life would be changed forever. He didn't want that. He liked his life and didn't want it to change. It felt as though he were at a road junction with two directions to travel in. One was safe and comfortable, the other was unknown, maybe even dangerous. He stood still, unable to decide as her running form disappeared into the night.

Then, his mind was made up for him.

Behind him, toward the village, a light appeared in the distance. It flickered and danced, casting long shadows along the road and creating shimmering reflections in the water that covered its surface. The warm glow illuminating the surroundings, revealing the silhouettes of trees against the night sky.

Something about the light made him feel uneasy. He couldn't walk to the village without walking towards the light. So, he had no choice. He picked up the remaining box and jogged after Lena.

When he eventually caught up with her, she had run all the way to his car. She was gesturing to him as he approached.

"Over here," she spoke urgently, ducking behind a tree.

Joining her, he saw she was unclasping the catches on the box she had carried. Reaching inside, she removed a long, metallic object.

"What's going on?" asked Carl once he had recovered his breath. "How come your ankle is okay? And what the hell is that light behind us?"

Lena crouched down and raised the metallic object to her shoulder.

"Get behind me and get the Spinker out of its crate, and I'll answer all your questions. You need to know what's going on."

"No shit!" answered Carl wryly. He watched as she sighted down what was obviously a weapon back down the road towards the village.

"Wait! Is that a weapon? What the fuck?" he exclaimed.

"This is a Koolu," she explained. "It's an energy discharge weapon, one of the latest models. We are going to be under attack soon. I really suggest that you get that Spinker out of its crate."

Carl laughed. He couldn't help himself, but when she didn't join in. He stopped.

"Your serious?"

"Yep," she replied without taking her eyes from the road. "You've probably realised by now that I'm not from around here."

"Well, yes, that had crossed my mind. But you can't carry a weapon without a permit." He paused. "At least I don't think you can. Wait! What's a Koolu? I've never heard of that."

"If you'd let me finish, I was trying to explain. While I do, get the Spinker."

Carl did as she asked and give her the time to explain. He unclasped the catches on the case.

"As I was saying, I'm not from around here, but I've been followed. I'm sure that they're still after me. Hence the weapons, which my colleague, Alec, sent to me. He also sent a Recharger. I used it to power up my psionic energy nodes. Now I'm at full strength. It was a simple matter to heal my injuries."

Carl gazed down at the compact black metal object in the crate while he tried to digest what Lena had just said. Nothing had changed his mind. He still thought she had a head injury. She was still talking complete rubbish, but he couldn't explain the crates and the fact that she could now run when a short time ago she could hardly walk. Could there be some truth in what she had said?

"Get down!" she shouted.

Carl instinctively ducked just in time. A projectile whizzed past where his head had been seconds ago. It made a buzzing sound as it flew by, leaving a faint orange trail.

"Shit!" he shouted as he threw himself to the ground. "What was that?"

"Bring the Spinker to me, but keep low and behind me," Lena instructed him urgently.

The time for disbelief was over. Carl obeyed the request. He reached up and pulled the black object from the crate and crawled on all fours to Lena, who reached behind her to take it from him. Without taking her eyes from the road, she set the object next to her and pressed a stud on its side.

Present Day

"What was the light, dad?" asked David.

"It was the enemy, silly," answered Phoebe.

"I know that!" replied David dismissively. "Tell us about the weapons, dad. Why did they have funny names?"

"I think the names are silly," said Phoebe.

"They are strange names," agreed Carl. "I suppose they might have been named after the people who invented them, but I didn't think to ask."

He was a little concerned that David seemed to be fixated on the weapons.

"You guys know that fighting is wrong, right?" he asked.

They both nodded solemnly, their big wide eyes staring up at him.

"This story isn't exactly PG rated you know. I shouldn't really be telling you."

"We know, dad," and answered David.

"We just like the witch," continued Phoebe.

"Yeah, she's awesome," said David.

Eight Years Ago

"What's happening?" asked Carl. "Who's shooting at us?"

He crouched next to Lena, following her gaze down the road, which was lit up by the flickering light.

"Just around that bend. If you look down this barrel, you'll see what I can see."

Carl leaned in close, following her instructions. Sure enough, she had an unobstructed view of the road and, sure enough; the light was coming from around a bend.

"What is it?" he whispered.

"We're not sure," she whispered back. "All we know is that they don't like us."

He leaned closer, their cheeks almost touching.

"You don't know? That sounds crazy."

She nodded. "Yes, it does." She smiled, but never once took her eyes from the light.

Carl turned to gaze at her profile, their faces only a breath apart. In the dim light of the misty rain filled night, he could make out every delicate feature of her face: the constellation of freckles that dusted her nose and cheeks like stars in the night sky, the strands of wet hair clinging to her forehead and framing her face. Her long eyelashes glistened with raindrops like tiny crystals.

"Like what you see?" she asked.

He moved away quickly, embarrassed at being caught.

"Sorry," he mumbled. "I didn't mean to stare, it's just…" he hesitated. "Things are a bit…"

"Strange," she completed his sentence. "I get it. Don't worry, I get it a lot."

"You have a high opinion of yourself!"

"With good reason."

Carl changed the subject. "So, what do we do now? Do we just wait?"

"Uh huh, they'll make a move soon."

"What do you want me to do?"

"Just stay behind me and don't interfere, no matter what happens."

"I'm glad you said that. Don't you worry. I'm afraid of guns."

He saw a small smile flicker at the edges of her mouth.

"So am I."

Present Day

"Are you really afraid of guns?" asked Phoebe.

"Yes, and so is any sensible person," replied Carl.

"Did you like the witch?" asked David.

Carl smiled.

"Wait till the end of the story to find out."

Eight Years Ago

They didn't have to wait long.

In the night's stillness, barely audible over the gentle tapping of the light rain, a humming sound that was almost melodic could be heard coming from the direction of the flickering light.

Carl felt Lena tense beside him. Both watching the road intently. It wasn't long before they saw movement. Curving around the bend, bathed in the flickering light from behind and casting a looming shadow on the road creeping towards them, floated a black cube about one metre on each side. It hovered about three metres above the ground, gliding with a slow and deliberate pace towards them. The surrounding air seemed to shimmer with a dark energy. It looked ominous and dangerous.

Lena jerked, and a blue streak sped from her weapon to impact the cube. Carl watched in fascination as the cube wobbled, dropped towards the road and then correct itself, resuming its height and steady progress towards them.

"Shit!" Lena cursed.

Carl watched as she pulled a lever back and pressed a stud on the side of her weapon. She aimed again and pulled the trigger. This time, the blue streak was brighter and lasted longer. It hit the cube as before, but whatever Lena had done, it had a profound effect on the cube. It dropped to the ground, rainwater and dirt splashing into the air. The humming stopped and everything was still.

Carl breathed a sigh of relief.

"Well done, you've killed it!"

Lena glanced sideways at him over the top of the weapon. He expected her to have a triumphant smile on her face, instead; she was serious.

"It's not over," she said grimly.

"But that thing's dead," he pointed out. "We should get out of here." He started to rise, but she griped his arm, pulling him back down.

"The light is still there," she inclined her head to the road.

He looked back down the road. She was right. The flickering light was still there.

Present Day

"What was that box thing, dad?" asked David.

"I don't know," Answered Carl. "But whatever it was, Lena killed it."

"With the Koolu," David pointed out.

"Yes, with the Koolu."

"Were you frightened?" asked Phoebe.

"Oh yes, very. Don't forget, it was dark and raining and the only light was coming from down the road. And then I was with this strange woman who was firing weapons. It was very scary."

Carl felt a tiny hand worm its way into his.

"Don't be scared, Dad," said Phoebe, her face serious. "We'll look after you."

David nodded in agreement.

Eight Years Ago

"What happens now?" asked Carl.

"We wait," answered Lena.

They were silent for a while, the only sound coming from the pattering of raindrops on the leaves and the ground.

"Can you get your friend Alec to come and help us?" asked Carl. "Can't he send some troops to help us?"

"It doesn't work like that."

"Why not?" hissed Carl. "Call him or whatever you do and tell him to get us out of here."

"We don't have the energy to do that," she explained. "Have you any idea how much energy it took to get me here?" She didn't wait for a reply. "I'll tell you. Three fusion reactors running at thirty gigawatts each, that's how much. Do you know how much that is?"

Carl shook his head.

"Nearly the entire energy output of the UK."

"Oh. I guess that's a lot."

There was silence again, each of them lost in their thoughts.

"So, what do you do?" asked Lena, breaking the silence.

"You mean for a job?" asked Carl. "I'm nothing special. I'm a history teacher."

"Teaching kids is special. How come you're out here so late at night?"

"I was driving home, when the flash caused me to drive onto the verge," he indicated his car that sat in the long grass and mud on the other side of the road.

"Pretty late for a teacher to be out."

"Yeah, well, I was on a date."

"Really?" Lena shot him a quick glance. "How did it go?"

Carl smiled ruefully. "Actually, I missed it." He caught her smiling as she continued her observation of the road.

"Oh dear, he or she won't be too happy."

"She was called Monica, if you must know. I'll have to face the music tomorrow, if I live through this."

"You and Monica are serious, then?"

"No, not at all. It was a blind date. My friends are all married and are trying to match me up. No luck so far."

"Sounds like fun."

"Nope, it's not. I'd rather meet someone accidentally."

Lena shot him another glance, a small smile on her lips.

"Like meeting me?" she asked.

Carl looked away and gave a short, muffled cough.

She faced the road again, her body suddenly tense.

"Movement," she breathed in an urgent tone. "Get ready."

"Ready for what? There isn't anything I can do!"

Present Day

"What's a fusion reactor, dad?" asked David.

"Well, we don't have them here, although there is a lot of research going on right now. From what I've read, it's harnessing the power of the Sun to generate electricity."

"Wow!"

"But the witch said she had three of them," Phoebe pointed out.

"Yes, she did," replied Carl. "I still didn't know where she had come from, but I figured it must be a long way away."

"Tell us the rest of the story, Dad. The aliens are going to attack again!"

"We don't know that they're aliens," replied Carl.

"What else could they be?" asked David.

Eight Years Ago

Another black cube appeared from around the bend in the road. It looked the same as the previous one. It was hovering as before, accompanied by the same melodic humming.

Lena wasted no time. She fired her weapon as before, but this time, although the cube wobbled, it didn't crash to the ground.

"Shit!" she exclaimed. "It's adapted!"

She fired repeatedly, blue fire splashing against its surface but not stopping its inexorable progress towards them.

"Do something!" shouted Carl.

His heart pounded in his chest, watching in horror as a whirling, glowing purple object hurtled towards them at breakneck speed. He barely had time to register it before it collided with an invisible barrier directly in front of them. The impact was deafening, a screeching noise that pierced his eardrums and echoed through the air. The ground beneath them shook violently and a massive crater, five meters wide, appeared in front of them. Chunks of earth and rocks flew into the air, raining down around them like deadly hail.

"What the fuck!" he screamed, throwing himself flat on the ground. From the corner of his eye, he saw Lena throwing her weapon to the ground. She picked up the Spinker and quickly fired it towards the approaching black cube.

A sudden, blinding flash of light illuminated the area, followed by an earth-shaking boom that left his ears ringing. More debris rained down from the sky, some of it slamming into the invisible force field with screeches and bursts of energy. The acrid smell of smoke and burning metal filled the air.

Holding his hands over his ears, Carl closed his eyes tight shut, trying to block out the surrounding chaos. After a few seconds, things were quieter, and he opened his eyes. It took a few more seconds to register that Lena was gone.

He yelled out her name, scrambling to stand up. It didn't take long to spot her - she was in the middle of the road, making her way towards the bend and the flickering light. With a fierce determination, she held the Spinker at her waist with both hands as she marched towards their enemy.

"Lena!" he shouted, but she ignored him and carried on towards the light.

What was she doing? Was she mad? She was walking directly towards the enemy, whoever they were. She was surely going to get herself killed. Should he run after her? He hesitated, unsure what to do, but then she rounded the bend and was gone.

Present Day

"She was very brave," said Phoebe.

"Did the Spinker kill the black cube thing?" asked David.

"I think so," replied Carl. "At least it wasn't there when I got up looking for Lena."

"It must have been awesome!" said David. "Kaboom! It blew into smithereens!"

"Well, it didn't feel awesome," Carl pointed out. "In fact, it was pretty scary."

"I wish I had been there to see it blown up."

Carl ruffled David's hair.

"I'm pretty glad that you weren't."

Eight Years Ago

A deafening explosion, larger than the last, ripped through the air and sent Carl tumbling to the ground. The impact of his back hitting the dirt knocked the wind out of his lungs. As he lay there, gasping for breath, he watched in awe as a colossal fireball erupted into the night sky. Its fierce orange glow illuminated the road and surrounding trees, casting an eerie light on everything it touched. The heat from the blast washed over him like a wave, causing him to shield his face with his arms. It was a sight that both terrified and captivated him, and he couldn't tear his eyes away from it.

As the light from the fireball slowly dimmed, and the darkness returned, he remembered Lena. She was surely dead. Nothing could have survived that.

With aching muscles, he slowly pushed himself off the ground and took in the sight of utter destruction around him. Trees lay splintered and felled, their branches torn and scattered across the ground. A thick layer of debris flattened bushes and foliage, with some still smouldering with embers. Trails of smoke rose into the air, casting a hazy veil over the desolate landscape. The once-clear road was now unrecognisable, replaced by a churned-up field that resembled a ploughed patch of earth. The scent of ash and burnt wood lingered in the air, a testament to the chaos and devastation that had just occurred.

"Holy shit!" he breathed.

What had just happened? An unexplained and overwhelming wave of sadness came crashing over him. It felt like a heavy weight, crushing his chest and making it hard to breathe. Lena was gone. Had she sacrificed herself to protect him? He had only known her for a brief time, but somehow, in the intense situation that they had found themselves in, he had felt close to her. And now she was gone.

By now it was almost pitch black, the explosion's light fading away. His phone had vanished in the chaos, and he had no way of finding it. Soon, he would be engulfed in complete blackness. He turned around, trying to figure out his next move, when he saw that miraculously, his car was undamaged.

Quickly, he strode over to it and sighed with relief when the interior light came on when he opened the driver's door. At least he had some light to banish the darkness, but he was still stuck. He was going nowhere. He collapsed into the driver's seat and rubbed at his face with his hands. What a night.

"Can I get a lift?" a voice called out from the darkness.

Startled, Carl quickly exited the car.

"Lena?" he called out, his voice full of emotion.

"Who else?" she replied as she appeared from the darkness to stand before him.

He couldn't help himself. Reaching forward, he pulled her to him and hugged her tightly. He was surprised when she returned the hug.

"I thought you were dead," he breathed into her hair.

She chuckled quietly, "Not likely. What do you say? Shall we get out of here?"

"I think that's a fucking great idea, but we're still stuck." Releasing her, he waved his arm behind him towards the car. She peered over his shoulder and grinned at him.

"That's not a problem. Here, hold this." She passed him the Spinker.

"What are you going to do?" he asked, holding the Spinker carefully.

She didn't answer. Instead, she raised her right hand and made a peculiar gesture. A shocked Carl watched as his car rose into the air to be placed gently back on the road.

Lena turned and beamed at him in triumph.

"Can we go now?"

Carl just gaped at her. "How did you do that?" he croaked.

She tilted her head to one side.

"Let's call it magic, shall we? Can we get going before the authorities come to investigate?"

She strolled to the other side of the car and slipped into the front passenger seat. As Carl watched her, he was struck by the sheer impossibility of what he had just witnessed. This woman, with her mysterious ways and surprising actions, had turned his life upside down. He could never forget what had happened tonight.

He sighed, walked up to the car, and got into the driver's seat.

"Where to?" he asked.

She turned and smiled at him her eyes sparkling.

"You know what? I would love a nightcap. How about we go to your place?"

Carl started the engine and put the car in gear.

Present Day

"Wow, that big explosion must have been massive," said David.

"Dad?" asked Phoebe. "Did you bring her to this house?"

"I did Pheebs," Carl replied with a smile.

"Hmmm," she replied, a distant look in her eyes.

"Tell us more about the explosion," urged David.

"I think that's enough for tonight. It's time for bed."

"Aww Dad, you said we could have a hot chocolate," whined Phoebe.

At that moment, their mother entered the room carrying two steaming mugs.

"Have you two rascals been giving your old dad a hard time?" she asked.

"Nah, he's been telling us the witch story," explained David, with a big grin plastered over his face.

Their mother's striking blue eyes locked onto her Carl's with a knowing look. Her elfin features accented by short, blonde hair cut in a sleek bob. The smattering of freckles across her nose and cheeks crinkled as she flashed a small smile.

"Not that old story again," she complained.

"Aww mum, we love it!" David protested.

"Yeah, mum, it's a great story," Phoebe chimed in.

Carl extracted himself from the tangle of his children and rose from the bed. As their mother handed out hot chocolate mugs to each child, they eagerly accepted them.

"Be careful not to spill anything," Carl warned. "We don't want to change the bedding."

"We won't," replied Phoebe with a determined expression, a chocolate ring around her mouth.

"So, you two like that story, huh?" their mother teased.

David nodded vigorously, almost spilling his hot chocolate.

"But she's not really a witch," he objected. "She's just a woman."

"Yes, she is!" Phoebe retorted furiously. "She's smart, strong, and beautiful!" She turned to look up at Carl with wide eyes, seeking confirmation. "Isn't that right, Dad?"

Carl beamed at Phoebe before her before wrapping his arm around Lena, drawing her closer. He gazed lovingly into her eyes.

"You're absolutely right, Phoebe. She's all that and more. She's incredibly bright, strong-willed, and very, very beautiful."

The Thought Collector

My name is Harvinder, and I am broken.

I lie in the darkness, staring at the ceiling, cursing my stupidity. I know what I must do, but I'm dreading it. I don't want to do it. I'm scared.

A single tear runs from the corner of one eye across my cheek. I don't wipe it away. Instead, I close my eyes and breathe in a quavering deep breath. I can't put it off much longer; I have to act. Ignoring it won't make it go away. I pull the bedsheet up to my chin and go over the events from the last few weeks. Could I have done anything different? Was it my fault?

It started almost exactly six weeks ago. I was involved in a traffic accident. An idiot driver swerved into the centre of the road to avoid a cyclist they hadn't seen. He hit me head-on. Fortunately, I wasn't going very fast, but the airbag deployed, fracturing my wrist and giving me a black eye. I didn't know it then, but much more damage was done.

It happened later that night after going to the Medical Bay for treatment. I was dropping off to sleep, dozing between reality and dreams, when suddenly I was someone else. I was still me, but not me.

I found myself in a room with a paintbrush in my hand. I knew I was in my studio and that I was a celebrated artist. My specialism was nudes where my interpretation of the naked form was applauded by critics and artists alike. My work was sold around the world for thousands of pounds. I was supremely confident and happy as I applied the brush strokes to the canvas, looking back and forth at the naked man, who was my model for the day.

After a while, I realised what had happened. Somehow, I had connected and entered the mind of a version of myself in another parallel world. She was one hundred percent me. Another Harvinder. But unlike me, she was successful. She was in her prime, a celebrated artist, well-known and respected in her world.

At the time, I didn't question how or why it had happened. I just revelled in the emotions and sensations flowing from my alternate self. She was so unlike me. And for a while, I was her. I felt her satisfaction and pleasure as she applied the paint. I admired the beauty of the naked man sprawled on the chaise longue. I could smell the paint and taste the cold coffee I occasionally sipped as I stepped back to view the progress of the painting.

It was glorious. I loved it. Every second of it. Eventually, I fell asleep. I dreamed of painting and naked men.

When I awoke in the morning, I puzzled over what had happened. An idea formed in my head. I raised my right hand and gazed at the cast. After the doctor reset the bones, she put them in a cast to keep them stable. She had been careful to ensure that the plaster did not cover the rings and bracelet of my Assist. It didn't take long before I found the issue. The bracelet had a tiny, almost imperceptible crack.

Realisation dawned. The car crash had damaged my Assist. The miracle instrument that boosted the powers of my mind must be malfunctioning. We all know about the multiverse, of course. The myriad of worlds that exist side by side. The defect was connecting me with alternate versions of myself in different worlds.

I knew I should report it. I should get a replacement. But the memories from the previous night were still fresh in my mind. They were powerful and irresistible. I craved to re-live those intense emotions, sensations, and feelings once more. So, I kept it to myself.

Over the next few weeks, I visited hundreds of versions of myself.

In one world, I was an exotic dancer, gyrating semi-naked on a stage, revelling in the sensuous nature of the dance and the roars of approval from the crowd. In another, I was a racing car driver, adrenalin pumping through my veins as I crossed the winning line. In one, I was a TV game host, introducing contestants and handing out prizes. In yet another, I was the lead singer in a heavy rock band, my vocals filling a stadium full of cheering fans.

My nights were filled with thrills, excitement, intrigue, love and laughter, all experienced through the lives of other versions of me. I collected them all. I stored away all the experiences to re-live them whenever I wanted.

Until one day, I met an evil version of myself.

She took me completely by surprise. I had just won a marathon; the exhilaration filling my tired body with endorphins, a massive smile on my face when I felt myself move into another version of me.

I was prepared to experience something new and exciting as usual. Instead, all I felt was hate and spite, and something else. Something that was most definitely not me. Greed. Coupled with a feeling of an insatiable appetite and craving. This version of me was different. She wasn't successful at the peak of her game like the others. She was scheming and avaricious.

And unlike all the others, she knew I was there!

None of the other versions of me had any idea that I joined with them. I was along for the ride, experiencing everything as though I were them. Never had a single one of them known I was there until now.

"I was wondering when you'd show up," she said, a hint of scorn in her thought.

I didn't know what to say. I was aghast at the horror I could see in her mind. It left me speechless and shocked.

"It was only a matter of time until Miss Goody two shoes appeared," she continued.

I couldn't answer.

"What's the matter? Lost your voice, little girl?" the thought sneered.

I said nothing; I was growing increasingly alarmed at what I could see in her mind. She was a monster.

"Well, I have things to do, people to kill," she laughed. *"I'd rather not have you watching, so get lost!"*

With that terrifying statement, she threw me out of her mind, and I found myself alone in my bed in the dark.

I lay there shaking. I couldn't stop the images I had seen in her mind replaying over and over. Some were truly horrible and looked like they came straight out of a horror movie. But I knew that wasn't the case. I knew they were all true. These images were things she had done. They weren't fake; they were real.

It took a while for me to recover. Eventually, I resorted to my ability to move memories away, where they couldn't dominate my thoughts, leaving me space to think.

Even then, I didn't realise the seriousness of the situation. Sure, I'd met my evil twin, but so what? It had been weeks before I fell into an evil mind; until then, every mind had been successful and exciting. I reasoned that the chances of meeting her again were close to zero.

So, I did nothing.

By the next night, I had dismissed the encounter as one in a million. I lay down on my bed and closed my eyes, a thin smile on my lips as I eagerly looked forward to another exhilarating experience.

That was when I realised my mistake.

I was once again in her body and watched with horror as she thrust a long, sharp knife up and into the chest of a small, defenceless woman. My malicious doppelgänger pulled the woman close, gazing deep into her eyes as they filled with pain and terror. I let out a scream and snapped my eyes open to see the dark ceiling above me. I had severed the connection but could still hear her cackling laughter echoing in my mind.

I rolled over to my side and threw up over the side of the bed. I couldn't stop the images, feelings, and sensations flashing through my mind. The woman's expression of agony and surprise. The hot blood running over my knife-hand. The glee and joy as I gazed into those shocked eyes.

It was the most horrendous thing I had ever experienced. It took me a long time to recover. The next day, I was useless. Trying to work was a waste of time. I couldn't stop thinking about what I had witnessed. Slowly, I came to the realisation that I had to do something. Even though this version of me lived in another parallel world, I couldn't let her carry-on murdering. I had to act.

So here I am. Back in my bedroom, lying on my bed, trying to drum up the courage to do what I must do.

Kill her.

I know it won't be easy. I've never killed before; the thought of it fills me with terror. I'm not even sure that I can do it. But I can't let her carry on killing; I just can't. How many people has she already killed? And how many will she kill in the future? I have to stop her. This is the only way I can think of to do that.

Steeling myself, I close my eyes and relax. After last night, I feel sure I'll end up with her, and sure enough, after a few short seconds, I'm there, inside her putrid mind. It's night-time. There's a fog, and she's walking down an unlit street searching for a new victim.

"Ah, you're back," she thinks at me.

How does she I'm here? None of my other duplicates did. Or did they?

"Did you enjoy the show?" she asks, chuckling to herself.

I'm disgusted and appalled. She seems to revel in my discomfort.

"Why?" I ask. "Why do you do it?"

She tosses her black hair to one side before answering.

"I enjoy it," she answers. "Didn't you feel a thrill as I plunged that blade into her chest?"

There's no reasoning with her. She is evil through and through. I must follow through with my plan. I feel the knife in her hand where she is hiding it beneath her jacket. I know that I have seconds to do it. Soon, she'll know what I know. She'll realise what I intend, and she'll stop me.

I flood my presence into her mind with sudden force. In a fraction of a second, I take control of her arm, holding the knife. I jerk it out from beneath her jacket and thrust it as hard as I can into her neck.

I feel her pain as I let go of my control. She screams in my head.

"You bitch!"

I am horrified at what I've done, but I know it was necessary. I've stopped her. I've done it! I feel her blood spurting out of her neck onto the pavement as she staggers sideways and slides down a wall.

"You think you've won?" her thought spits venom. "You think you've stopped me?"

I wonder what she's talking about, but I dismiss her ramblings. She's dying, her blood pooling beneath her.

"*You'd better be on the lookout,*" she seethes at me. "*I'll get you for this.*"

She can't get me. She'll be dead soon.

"*Do you think I'm the only one?*" she asks, her thoughts growing faint. "*Don't you know what you've done?*"

I puzzle over her words. I have no idea what she's talking about.

"*There are many versions of me,*" she continues. "*There'll be some that survive your cowardly attack. They know who you are. They'll come after you. You're as good as dead!*"

As she dies, I leave her world and arrive back in my own.

Her words hit me.

She was right. That's how the multiverse works. There will be hundreds of others like her, maybe thousands. By killing her, I'd killed myself!

Delivery

Day One.

I open the door to reveal a delivery driver. He's a young man wearing a cap, and a brown jacket which looks like a uniform. In his hands, he has a small, brown parcel.

"Hi," he says, his smile breaks into a grin. I grit my teeth as his eyes travel from my face to linger on my chest. "Would you mind holding this parcel for your neighbour love?"

My eyes flick from his to the parcel that he's holding out to me. It's small, maybe only six inches square.

"It's for number four," he continues, his eyes never leaving my chest.

"Sure," I reply, reaching for the parcel, more to stop him looking at me than anything else. He hands me the parcel and pulls out a notepad. He scribbles on it.

"I'll leave them a card," he explains.

"Okay," I answer, closing the door without waiting for him to reply. The catch snicks shut, and I turn the key. I lean back against it, sighing. Men are all bastards. I don't care that we live in a modern society and we're all equal. The fact is, we aren't. Men are always looking at me, cracking jokes and I'm sure most of them think they're better than me.

After placing the package onto the table next to the door, I return to the living room, where I drop onto the couch and grab my glass of wine. With a click of the remote, the romantic movie continues from where it had paused. I curl up on the couch, tucking my feet underneath me, covering myself with a cosy blanket.

Day Two.

I head out to work, but before I get in my car, I walk across the street and down two houses. I knock on the door of number four. As I wait for someone to answer, I look at the name on the parcel - Dawn Williams. I don't know her. But then I don't know any of my neighbours, I like to keep to myself. I don't enjoy socialising.

No one answers the door, so I knock again. I wait, but there's still no answer. Dawn, or anyone else who lives here, is obviously not home. I walk back to my house, get into my car, and drive to work.

Work is boring as usual. I'm the Personal Assistant to the Chief Executive Officer of a small insurance company. He's not in, visiting a branch nearby or playing golf, so there isn't much for me to do.

At lunch, I sit with some colleagues in the canteen.

"Have you heard? There's been another unexplainable death in the town."

David is his usual lively self, his hand gestures adding to his dramatic flair. He's openly gay and my closest friend, and perhaps the only one I have. As an introvert, I prefer my own company and find solace in solitude. Being around people often makes me feel anxious and overwhelmed.

"How many is that now?" asks Diane. She's picking at her salad, clearly not enjoying it.

"Twelve!" replies David. He leans forward over the table, his tie falling onto his pizza. "I think we have a serial killer," he whispers conspiratorially.

"Twelve deaths do not a serial killer make," Amira chipped in.

"Yes, it does!" retorted David.

"For starters, the police would have informed the public." As Amira speaks, she ticks off her points one by one on the fingers of her right hand. "It would be all over the news and in the papers, and finally the MO would be the same."

"MO?" asks David. He sits back in his chair, a pout on his lips.

"The pattern and method used to kill. Serial killers usually use the same method to kill their victims," explains Amira. "From what I've heard on the news, there's nothing to connect the deaths. They look unrelated."

"That's what they want you to think!" scoffs David.

I tune out and finish my sandwich. I'm not interested in the conversation.

At five pm, I pack up and drive home. It's been a long day and I can't wait to have a bath, but as I pull up onto my driveway and turn off the engine, I see the parcel for number four on the passenger seat. I close my eyes and sigh. I can't be bothered, but I can't keep their parcel.

I exit the car, package in hand, and stride across the road towards number four. I do my best to ignore my idiot next-door neighbour who is peering out through a window. He's a creep. I hate the way he's always looking at me. He always grins and tries to engage me in a conversation, and I always ignore him.

I knock on the door of number four once more. After a while, it slowly opens, and I am struck by the sight before me. A woman stands in the doorway. Her beauty takes my breath away. I can't help but wonder why I haven't seen her around before. Could she be new to the neighbourhood? I don't recall seeing any moving vans.

She's dressed in comfortable leisure wear, dark blue leggings hugging her every curve, and a black crop top clings enticingly to her breasts. The fabric seems to mould to her body, accentuating her figure. It's the perfect blend of comfort and style, making her stand out as a confident and fashionable person.

Long, sleek black hair frames her face, and her evenly tanned complexion enhances her delicate features. She gazes at me. Her dark eyes seem to burn with a fierce intensity, sparking with energy and curiosity. She welcomes me with a smile, her perfectly shaped lips turned upward, exuding amusement or perhaps appreciation.

I'm speechless and completely forget why I'm at her door.

"Is that for me?" she asks, her smile dazzling. I feel like an idiot for staring at her in awe. She points to the package I'm holding, the fingers of her right hand adorned with golden rings.

I lower my gaze to look at what I'm carrying. The spell breaks and I remember why I'm here.

"Yes." My voice is only just audible and hoarse. I'm shocked at how pathetic it sounds. I clear my throat. "Are you Dawn?"

She nods enthusiastically. "That's me." She pauses and tilts her head to one side. "I'm new, only moved in three weeks ago. I don't think I've seen you before. Which one is you?" She looks across the road at the houses opposite.

"Number ten," I reply. As she nods, I hand her the small package. When she takes it from me, our fingertips brush and I feel a small thrill of electricity course through my hand and up my arm. I step back in shock, my eyes going wide. She appears not to notice.

"Thanks," she says. "What's your name?"

"Michelle," I reply automatically, without thinking.

"Well Michelle, I guess I'll be seeing more of you?"

I blush, my cheeks and neck feeling as hot as the summer sun. My god, what's happening to me? This isn't me. I'm not a sixteen-year-old girl. Why am I so affected by this woman? But of course, I know the answer. She's gorgeous and just my type. I mumble a reply, turn and walk away, conscious of her eyes boring into my back.

The creep is still there, standing at his window, watching as I walk past.

Day Three.

The next day drags at work as usual. Today, I have a lot of work to do, but somehow, I can't concentrate and end up watching YouTube videos and Facebook reels. I sink further and further into boredom. The hours creep by at a snail's pace, each minute feeling like an eternity. I am relieved when the clock finally strikes five pm.

On the way home, I stop at a Chinese to pick up some noodles. When I get home, I change into my most comfortable pyjamas and settle down on the couch with the noodles and a glass of wine to watch a movie. Just as the dramatic intro music ends and the plot begins to unfold, the doorbell rings, breaking the peaceful atmosphere with a jolt.

When I open the door, it's the same delivery driver as the other day.

"Hello love. Will you take this package for number four again?" He smiles at me, with what I'm sure he thinks is his best winning smile. I scowl at him.

I'm not swayed by his charm. "I am not your love," I retort, snatching the package from his outstretched hand before slamming the door in his face. Men like him infuriate me with their presumptuous attitudes, thinking a simple smile is all it takes to win me over. Their arrogance makes me angry.

I frown at the carefully wrapped brown package. It's addressed to Dawn and is exactly the same size and weight as the previous one. It looks like she's ordered a duplicate of whatever was in the first one. When I shake it near my ear, there's no rattling. Whatever is inside, it's not loose.

I place it on the table in the hall and go back to the film, annoyed by the interruption.

Day Four.

It's Saturday, my day for doing absolutely nothing. I like to lie in, get up when I want to, laze around all day, watching TV, eating when I want to eat, reading and playing games. So, I'm really annoyed when the doorbell rings when I'm still in bed.

I roll onto my side and glance at the clock on the bedside table. The numbers read nine thirty-three. Too early to start the day. I close my eyes, hoping whoever is at the door will go away if I ignore them. But they don't. The doorbell continues to ring, its piercing sound unrelenting, making me more and more angry.

Eventually, I throw the bedclothes back angrily and stomp down the stairs. Wrenching the front door open, I realise my mistake. I forgot to throw on a robe. I'm standing in the doorway wearing a short T-shirt emblazoned with a grinning cartoon cat and nothing else.

"Wow! I thought I'd being seeing more of you, but not until we've been on a couple of dates!"

Dawn stands before me, a sly grin on her face. Her tight top has the words 'Don't fuck with me!' written across her chest in bold white letters, while her shorts cling to every curve, leaving little to the imagination. As she waits for me to respond, she licks her lips, her small pink tongue flicking in and out teasingly.

Embarrassment floods through me, leaving my face flushed and my body tense. I tug on the hem of my T-shirt, trying to cover myself up as much as possible. Ignoring my discomfort, she smiles at me with casual ease.

"You have a parcel for me?" she asks.

Her confidence only makes me feel more self-conscious in my near nakedness.

"Yes," I croak, and automatically reach for the small package on the table next to the door and hand it to her. I retreat to stand behind the door and peer around it at her.

"Thank you," she says, taking the package from me and watching me move to hide myself behind the door.

"I'm having a party tomorrow night." She purses her lips. "Well, not a party, just a get together with a few friends. Would you come if I asked you?"

She arches her eyebrows, anticipating my response. I'm still flustered by being in my nightclothes at the door. I've never been a fan of parties; socializing and making small talk have never been my strong suits.

"Tomorrow is Sunday," I blurt out.

She grins that dazzling smile of hers. "Yes," she replies. "Is that a problem?"

"Well, I work on Monday."

She looks at me with a quizzical expression on her face, as though she doesn't understand.

"Stay as long as you like, even if it's only five minutes." She pauses. "I'd really like you to come." She says it with meaning. There's an almost pleading tone to her voice that's mixed with something else. Something like excitement and anticipation.

I'm at a loss for words. I really hate parties, but I can't turn down her invitation. But also, I don't want to say yes.

"I'll think about it," I answer.

Her face lights up with a radiant smile and she clutches the package to her chest.

"Great!" She's clearly excited. Why, I can't imagine. "I'll see you tomorrow."

Day Five - AM.

I'm wearing my usual loose-fitting athletic attire as I jog along the footpath. They make me hot and sweaty, but it's just part of the deal. I wear them to avoid attention. Of course, the creep neighbour from next door has his eyes on me. He's constantly watching, and it makes my skin crawl as I pass by his house, setting off on my run.

It's not unusual to pass other runners or, more likely in my case, other runners pass me. So, I'm not surprised to hear footsteps approach from behind. I move to one side of the path to let them pass, but I'm shocked when Dawn appears, running beside me.

She's not like me. Instead of covering up, she's wearing tight fitting red lycra shorts and a matching crop top which was little more than a sports bra. She's topped it off with a black baseball cap and a pair of dark sunglasses.

Her long, tanned legs effortlessly keep pace as she turns to smile at me.

"Morning lovely," she says, hardly out of breath.

I'm breathing heavily and can barely manage a reply.

"Uh, morning," I gasp.

"Got anymore parcels for me?" she asks.

I shake my head, trying to breathe.

"I'm in all afternoon if one arrives." She pulls the rim of her cap down lower. "I'm looking forward to seeing you later, all dressed up." She looks me up and down. "See yah." She effortlessly speeds away, her toned legs powering her forward, her shorts hugging her shapely rear. I can't help but watch as she goes.

Later, I've showered and am preparing lunch when the doorbell rings.

Once again, it's the same delivery man and once again he has a delivery for Dawn. It looks like the others. That's three identical packages and I can't help but wonder what they are, and why do they keep coming to me?

It looks like I'll have to attend Dawn's party even if it's only to hand over the third package.

Day Five - PM.

I can't decide what to wear.

My wardrobe is full of beige tops, there's very little colour. I'm not a colourful person. I prefer to blend in, not stand out. There's a small part of me that would like to impress Dawn. I'm not good at picking up on signals, so I could be mistaken; I can't help thinking that she might be a little attracted to me. That just makes things worse. I want to look attractive, but it's not in my nature and to top it off, my clothes are all drab.

Really, there is only one option: the bridesmaid's dress.

Three years ago, I was a bridesmaid at my sister's wedding. She insisted that all her bridesmaids wear a summer dress. Although it's not really my thing, I wore it because that's what she wanted. It's cream with a blue floral pattern. It has short sleeves and a low-cut neckline, both of which I really don't like, but at least it's long and doesn't expose my legs.

Dawn hadn't given me a time to arrive, so I wait until seven and then walk to her door. The creep was there, watching me as always. This time he's standing in his front garden, a lecherous grin plastered all over his face as his eyes follow me walking past. I ignore him, even when he calls out.

"Nice evening. Going for a walk?"

I'm relieved to arrive at Dawn's door. The sooner I'm out of his gaze, the better. Butterflies dance in my stomach as I wait for the door to open. Then my thoughts race. What was I doing? This was so out of character. Did I really think that there was a possibility of me and Dawn getting together? The whole situation is ridiculous. And besides, there will be people here. Dawn had said that it was a party. I hate parties with a passion. This is silly. Suddenly, I change my mind about being here, and turn to leave.

"You came!"

I turn at the sound of Dawn's voice. She's standing in the doorway, dressed in a little black dress that hugs her curves and clings perfectly to her figure. The fabric glistens and sparkles, highlighting every contour of her body. She stands confidently, with her head held high and a subtle smirk playing on her lips. It's clear that she knows she looks stunning, and she revels in it.

"You look lovely," she says, her eyebrows raised and her eyes sparkling.

As before, I struggle to find words in her presence. It's not just because she's beautiful; there's something about her that commands attention. Something intangible that defies explanation.

Numbly, I hold out the package.

"Ah!" She takes it from me. "This one is special."

She moves back into the hallway and gestures for me to come inside.

"Come on in. Let me introduce you to some really nice people."

I automatically step forward, but my heart sinks. I don't want to be introduced to anyone. The thought makes me cringe inside.

I follow her into the lounge, trying hard to control my rising anxiety and wondering what's going to happen, because I've noticed something a little strange already; there's no music, and no raised voices, as there would normally be at a party.

"Everyone, this is my new friend, Michelle," Dawn announces as we enter the room.

I am taken aback by the small group in front of me - only four, two women and two men. They're all lounging on the furniture, their bodies sprawled out in a state of relaxation. The over-sized, cream sofas seem to engulf them. Their postures vary. - one woman lies on her back, arms folded behind her head; another, rests on her side, propped up by an array of colourful pillows. The two men slouch against the cushions, with their legs splayed out in front of them. It is as if they have no care in the world, content to relax and enjoy each other's company.

I'm greeted by four smiles and a variety of "Hi," "Hello," and "Nice to meet you." I just nod. What sort of party is this? Are they on drugs? My anxiety hits an all-time high. I don't like the way this is going. I now regret my decision to come even more.

"What would you like to drink?" asks Dawn. She touches my arm lightly.

The hairs on the back of my neck rise and my heart thumps wildly as I let her guide me to the kitchen. Her touch has a powerful effect on me.

"Wine?" I ask while trying desperately to think of how to get out of here as soon as possible. I'm out of my depth. Dawn's intoxicating presence is making it difficult to think, and I'm frightened about what might be happening in the lounge.

She hands me a glass of white wine and I take a big gulp.

"I guess things might seem a bit strange to you," says Dawn, eying me over her own glass as she takes a delicate sip. I take another gulp and nod.

"A bit."

She smiles.

"You find it difficult to be with people and make friends?"

I grimace and empty the glass. She reaches behind her to pick up a bottle and refills my glass.

"I was like you once," she continues. "Hard to believe, I know," she gives a little chuckle. "But it's true."

I can feel the wine's effect on me as I take a small sip.

"I avoided social situations and kept to myself as much as I could." She places the bottle on the countertop and slowly steps towards me.

"I used to cover myself by wearing loose-fitting, baggy clothes. I hated my body, and I hated people judging me."

She is so close that I can smell her perfume, then she takes one more step and our noses are inches apart. My heart races and my breathing quickens. I lick my dry lips, unable to take my eyes from hers.

Gently, she reaches up and unfastens my hair from its clip, allowing it to cascade down onto my shoulders. She leans forward and whispers in my ear.

"Then something amazing happened and everything changed."

I am rooted in place, unable to move, completely enchanted by her. Her voice is soothing as she speaks, and I can feel the warmth of her breath on my ear.

She whispers, her lips grazing my neck as she moves closer. "I have a gift for you," she says, her breath leaving a trail on my skin.

By now I'm trembling uncontrollably. I am completely overwhelmed by her. Then, suddenly, she steps back, and I'm left breathless. She turns to the countertop, picks up something, and then turns back to me. She's holding the package I gave to her earlier.

"This is the gift," she explains. "With this, you can be whoever you want to be, do whatever you want to do, get whatever you want."

It takes a moment for me to regain my composure and comprehend her words. I furrow my brow, confused and not understanding what she is saying.

"What do you mean?" I ask.

She smiles one of her captivating smiles.

"It will transform you and allow you to become the real you," she explains.

I take another drink from my glass, draining it for the second time. The alcohol is taking effect and I feel a little woozy. I wonder if she's drunk or maybe high on drugs because she is talking nonsense. I shake my head.

"I think it's time for me to go," I say, placing the glass on the countertop.

My heart skips a beat when I see the disappointment etched on her face. She looks so sad, so dejected that I step towards her, raising a hand to her shoulder. But I stop myself before I touch her.

"Don't go," she says in a small voice. "I didn't mean to frighten you."

I'm not sure what to say. She's different. The confident woman seems to have disappeared, and I can't help but wonder if this is who she used to be before something changed her. She reminds me of. Of. Me! I can't help myself. I grip her shoulder and squeeze.

She flashes me a thin, uncertain smile and I smile back. We lock gazes and something passes between us. It's a kind of recognition, of understanding, or realisation that we are, in fact, very similar.

She reaches across her chest and lays her hand on mine, which is still on her shoulder. We grin at each other. Something is different between us. We both feel it, I can tell. Where it will lead, I don't know.

I flick my gaze to the brown parcel in her other hand.

"What is it?" I ask.

Instead of answering, she hands it to me. I accept it from her and rip away the brown paper. Underneath, there is a black velvet box with a hinge on one side. It looks like a ring box, but a lot larger.

I look up at Dawn. Her bright eyes are sparkling with anticipation as she watches me. A small smile plays on her lips. I can tell she's excited for me to open the box.

I really hope that it contains nothing expensive. I would find that really embarrassing. It would be worse than being given flowers on a first date with someone I barely know. We're just neighbours, and as much as I might want it to be more, it's too early for that kind of gesture.

I lift the lid, and a gasp escapes my lips when I see what's inside. Neatly arranged on foam padding are many gold rings.

I shut the lid with a snap.

"I can't accept this," I say forcefully. My worst fear has become a reality.

Dawn grips the wrist of my hand holding the box.

"You can," she hisses. "I know what it looks like, me offering you a gift like this. I need you to trust me. These rings are special. If you would put them on, you'll understand."

I raise my gaze to meet hers. She's watching me intently, her eyes filled with longing and hope. I lower my eyes back to the box, and I notice something peculiar. I notice that each finger of Dawn's hand, which still holds my wrist, is adorned with a solitary gold ring.

Something clicks in my mind.

"Wait a minute," I gasp. "Are your rings the same?"

"Yes!" Dawn exclaims excitedly. "We all have a set."

I look towards the kitchen doorway.

"You mean your friends in the lounge?"

She nods and I frown, puzzled.

"Why?"

I watch her hesitate. Her gaze travels around the room, she releases my wrist; she picks up her glass of wine and takes a sip. She refocuses her attention on me and flashes an uncertain smile. Clearly unsure of what to say, she appears to be nervous. She leans back on the countertop and takes another drink. I'm not sure that she's going to answer my question.

"You don't have to answer," I say. "But I don't understand why you would give these to me." I gesture with the box towards her. I give her a little smile. "Unless you're trying to impress me or get in my pants!"

The wine has made me more talkative than usual. I can't believe what I just said, and I'm embarrassed. My eyes drop to the floor in shame. Slowly, she takes the box from me, and she wraps her arm around my shoulders. She is warm and soft, and her perfume is lovely. Without thinking, I wrap my arms around her tightly, pulling her close. It feels like coming home. I breathe in her scent, close my eyes and feel myself relax.

After a short time, Dawn loosens her embrace and steps back. I watch as she opens the box and removes the rings. I am surprised when I see each one has tiny delicate gold chains joining them together. She takes my hand and gazes deeply into my eyes. I meet her gaze and allow her to slide each ring onto a different finger on my right hand.

As she slips the last one onto my little finger, something happens.

A wave of emotions washes over me: excitement, anticipation, longing, and desire. My eyes widen in surprise, but before I can react, Dawn pulls me into a tight hug. She buries her head in my neck, and it takes a few moments for me to understand what's happening. These feelings aren't mine; they belong to her.

My thoughts are a jumble, tangled and twisted as my emotions collide with hers. They merge in a chaotic dance, like a tangled ball of twine fighting to unravel. Each one crashes into my mind in rapid succession - fear, worry, anticipation, desire - until finally I find a sense of calm amidst the storm. It's like riding a rollercoaster, with highs and lows and twists and turns that leave me breathless and exhilarated all at once. I feel calmed by her presence, and I know we are now connected in a way that can never be explained to anyone else.

She lifts her head and leans back to look deeply into my eyes.

"Now you see?" she whispers, our noses almost touching.

"Yes," I breathe. "What is it?"

She smiles. She's back to her confident self.

"It's called an Assist. It allows us to connect in new and deeper ways. Do you like it?"

"I'm not sure," I reply honestly. "It's overwhelming."

Her smile broadens.

"It is," she answers, her smile turning coy. "There's more to come." She holds up another set of rings. "These go on your toes." She flutters her eyelashes.

"There's more?"

"Oh, yes." She kisses the tip of my nose. "I think we should take it upstairs, don't you?"

A flutter of excitement dances within my chest, causing my heart to beat faster. A rush of heat floods my body, and my cheeks burn. My skin tingles and my palms grow sweaty. I'm unable to answer her. My gaze fixes on the deep pools of her dark eyes, mesmerised by their intensity. She interprets my silence as agreement and slowly pulls me towards the door. Every step feels electric, as though we are about to embark on something new and thrilling together.

Day Six.

Standing naked at the bedroom window, I watch the street below. It's early morning, and the sun is just appearing over the rooftops of the houses to my left. Behind me, I hear Dawn stirring in the king-size bed we shared last night. The memory of our lovemaking lingers, it fills me with a sense of euphoria and contentment that goes beyond physical pleasure. Last night was an experience that transcended mere sex.

She had slipped the extra set of shimmering gold rings on the toes of my left foot, while murmuring words I couldn't understand. Suddenly, it wasn't just our bodies that joined, but our minds as well. A connection unlike any other flooded my senses, binding us in a way that I had never experienced before. It was a feeling beyond words, beyond comprehension. And in that moment, I knew we were meant to be together forever.

It had happened so fast, but it had felt so right. But last night, when our minds connected, I saw how Dawn had engineered the whole thing. I hadn't noticed that the delivery man had the identical rings on his right hand. Worse, I didn't even recognise him when she had introduced me to her friends in the lounge last night. He was one of them, one of her group.

I felt her come up behind me when she slides her arms around my waist, pressing herself into my back.

"Morning lovely," she murmured into my neck.

"Morning," I smile back.

"Whatcha doing?" she asked.

"Watching my creep neighbour," I answer, holding onto her hands around my waist and leaning back into her.

"What's he doing" she asked as we watch him walk about in his front garden.

"He's waiting for me," I reply. "He knows when I go for my morning run. He's always there watching me and trying to talk to me. I always ignore him."

"He makes you uncomfortable?"

I nod.

"You know, you could do something about that."

"Confront him, you mean? I'm not sure it would make any difference."

She chuckles behind me, kissing the back of my head.

"You can do much more than that, my lovely. Why don't you get rid of him?"

I pull her hands away and turn to face her, shocked.

"You mean kill him! Do you know what you're saying?"

She puts her hands on my shoulders and holds me at arm's length.

"You don't have to let anyone bother you or make you uncomfortable anymore. You shouldn't have to put up with anything like that. Now that you're wearing your Assist, you can do something about it."

I'm shocked that she could even consider suggesting murder and I realise that even with our extraordinary connection of minds and bodies last night, there are still things I don't know about her.

"No one would ever find out," she continues. "It's simple to do. I can't say that it's painless for the victim, but then they all deserve it."

My mouth drops open as I understand what she's saying.

"You've already done it," I whisper. "You've killed someone!"

She nods, a serious look on her face.

"Yes, and they all had it coming."

Suddenly, my mind makes a connection, thoughts clicking together like puzzle pieces fitting into place.

"The unexplained deaths in the city," I gasp. "They were down to you!"

She nods once more.

"Either me or members of the group. Does that surprise you? I know you've thought of doing it yourself."

For a moment I'm speechless, my mouth opening and closing like a goldfish.

"But why? How?" I squeak.

"With this." She holds up her right hand, the gold rings glinting in the sunlight streaming through the window.

"And as to why," she looks me in the eye. "I think you know why."

She pulls at my shoulder, spinning me around to face the window once again. She stands close and points through the window.

"Look at him." She gestures at my creep of a neighbour. "You said it yourself. He's out there waiting for you to open your front door. And we both know why. He's obsessed with you. He probably fantasises about you. In his twisted mind, he believes that one day you'll talk to him, go out on a date, and eventually end up in his bed."

She's right. He's always been strange, and I've never liked the way he looks at me. I watch him as he pretends to pull up some weeds in his front garden, his gaze flicking up at regular intervals to the door of my house.

"He's the kind of man that will end up killing or raping someone," continues Dawn. "You know I'm right. Don't you think that the world would be a better place without him?"

I do sort of agree with her. There's always been something off about him. I could easily see him exposing himself and eventually escalating to committing sexual assault.

"Maybe," I reluctantly agree with her. "But killing someone?" I shuddered. "Please tell me you're not serious and you're joking."

She puts her arm across my shoulders and pulls me to her.

"It's not easy," she admits. "And it's not something I would normally condone, but sometimes there's no choice."

I turn to her.

"You've had to make that choice?" I ask.

In answer, she reaches up and caresses my cheek.

"Let me show you."

In an instant, alien thoughts, memories and feelings flood my mind as Dawn shares what happened to her two years earlier.

A cry of anguish escapes my lips and tears stream down my face as I am flooded with the intense emotions and pain from Dawn's memories. I instinctively wrap my arms around her, desperate to offer her comfort. The weight of what she has shared hits me like a physical blow, and it is almost too much to bear.

We hold onto each other, both sobbing uncontrollably. What she had experienced was the most horrible thing I could ever imagine. After a while, I recover a little.

"You killed him?" I ask with a trembling voice.

She nodded.

I take a deep tremulous breath and turn back to the window. My neighbour is still there, no longer pretending to be busy. He's staring intently at the door of my house.

"Show me," I tell her in a quiet voice.

Dawn knows what I mean. She smiles a small smile, tears glistening on her cheeks.

Adam

A rock, or something sharp, digs into my ribs, but I ignore it and focus on controlling my breathing. From my vantage point, two thousand meters away, I see him enjoying himself with his friends. He holds a glass of wine in one hand and gestures wildly with the other, clearly telling a story that he and his friends find hysterical.

He won't be laughing for long.

It's like watching a movie without the sound. I watch as he moves around the balcony, greeting guests with a handshake or clapping them on their backs. He's happy, but then why wouldn't he be? It's his birthday, and he's rich. He kisses a statuesque woman on her cheek. She's dressed in a little black dress, a sharp contrast to his white linen suit.

It won't be white for long.

By now, there's about twenty-five people on the balcony and they're all seating themselves at tables. Waiters and waitresses appear, topping up glasses and taking orders. He sits next to the tall woman, handing his panama hat to one of his security guards. There are two of them, their slightly bulging dinner jackets concealing shoulder holsters. They're both professional, well-muscled and relaxed.

They won't be relaxed for long.

A waiter brings in a large birthday cake on a trolley, expertly wheeling it around the tables and guests. There are lit candles on the cake, too many to count, but I know that there are seventy-four.

Everyone is singing and then clapping as the waiter cuts the cake and hands him a slice on a white china plate. It's a big slice.

He won't be eating it for long.

I check my watch. Two minutes. The Client was very specific. The target must die at a precise time. I didn't ask why; I don't care. The Client often has strange requests. Sometimes it's the method, sometimes it's a location and sometimes, like now, it's a specific time.

I flick the safety off on my AXSR .300 sniper rifle and relax, entering that Zen state that allows me to laser focus on the task. My eyes un-focus slightly and I feel an aura of calm descend upon me. I breathe in the crisp, cool air, listening to the cheerful chirping of birds in the distance. My elbows rest on the rough groundsheet beneath me and I can feel the warmth of the rifle stock against my cheek.

One minute later, my focus returns and I look through the telescopic sight. He's standing at the head of his table, obviously giving a speech. I move the crosshairs to centre on his ear. Despite the time requirements from The Client, I wait. At this distance, the bullet can take up to four seconds to arrive at the target. I need to make sure that he's relatively still or I might miss. Seated would be best. I'll only get one shot. His protection team will spring into action quickly, pulling him to the ground and shielding him with their bodies. I need to ensure that I hit the target with a single shot.

Waiting is something I'm very good at. A few minutes while he finishes his speech is nothing and soon, I see him sit. As soon as he leans back in his chair, I squeeze the trigger slowly until the rifle bucks against my shoulder. The sound of the bullet exploding from the barrel and then breaking the sound barrier echoes in my ears, even through the protection of my ear plugs.

It's with grim satisfaction that I see his head explode, blood, brain and flesh showering the guests seated at his table. There's pandemonium amongst the guests. I watch as they stream from the balcony, pushing and shoving at each other, desperate to get under cover and out of harm's way. One member of his protective team is cradling the target's body, the other has drawn his hand weapon and is staring in my direction.

I'm not worried. He can't see me, and he certainly can't hit me with a hand weapon at this range. I note with some regret that the tall woman in the black dress is also dead, her body slumped onto the table. The bullet must have struck her after passing through the target.

It's time to go. They'll throw everything into the search for me. Helicopters, dogs, police and troops will be here in minutes.

Making sure that the empty cartridge is on the groundsheet, I fold back the rifle's bipod legs. Then I carefully place it in the centre of the sheet and roll it up into a bundle. Grabbing my backpack and unzipping the front pocket, I pull out a red plastic bottle. Removing the cap, I spray the liquid from the bottle all over the surrounding ground, making sure to cover every surface that was touched by my hands and weapon with its corrosive contents.

I wouldn't be leaving even the most microscopic specimen of DNA.

The ground is still smouldering and bubbling as I pick up the groundsheet bundle. I quickly spray the area where the groundsheet had been and where I had just been lying.

It's time to leave.

I have no idea how the rings work, but I know how to use them. I've done this hundreds of times before, but each time I'm always amazed.

I close my eyes, concentrate and touch my fingers to my thumb on my right-hand one by one in the sequence I've learned, the rings and chains tinkling as my fingers move rapidly. When I open my eyes, I'm in the safe house.

I need to hurry. Even though I've taken as many precautions as I can, it's still possible that the authorities might trace me. I can't allow that. I approach the barrel, which sits incongruously in the corner of the room. Unsnapping the lid, I throw in the groundsheet bundle and watch as it sinks into the acid. Carefully, I lower my backpack into the boiling liquid, then I remove my clothes, including my watch, and throw them in to join the now dissolving contents. On the table next to the barrel, I flick a switch on a small panel. A timer starts to count down from thirty. I have that many seconds to exit the house before the explosives reduce it to rubble.

Once more I concentrate and move my fingers in that exact sequence that allows me to travel to anywhere that I can visualise. I arrive at the second safe house, unlike the other, which was still in the US. This one is in China. It's all part of my plan and it's the reason I've never been caught and never will. In this location, I shower and put on brand new clothes. I make two more jumps, each one to different countries and in each one, I make sure that there is nothing that can be traced to me. Each location is completely destroyed.

My final jump is to my current home, and I can finally relax.

The first thing I do is make myself a strong drink. Then I sit at my computer and pull up the proprietary messaging service that I use to communicate with The Client. There's a message waiting.

"You were not supposed to terminate the girlfriend."

I chuckle to myself and take a sip of my drink, the ice tinkling in the glass. The girlfriend was unavoidable. Sure, it was unintended, but given the exact time The Client wanted the target killed, I had to pull the trigger when I did. Of course, I missed The Client's specified time by a few seconds, but that too was unavoidable. I set the glass down and started typing.

"She was collateral damage, an unfortunate occurrence."

The reply was quick.

"I don't like unfortunate occurrences."

"In my profession, they happen," I type after taking another sip from the cold amber liquid in my glass.

"The unfortunate occurrence has caused problems that could have been avoided. One million will be deducted from your payment. Make sure that it doesn't happen again. A new contract will be forwarded to you shortly."

I'm not angry or surprised at The Client's response. The deduction of one million isn't going to affect the total payment much and I have plenty of money. Besides, money is not the reason I do this job. It doesn't take long to check my bank balance, and sure enough, the money has been deposited.

Closing the computer down, I drain my glass, walk into the bedroom and collapse onto the bed. It's been a long day, and it's not long before I fall asleep.

When I wake, it's the middle of the afternoon the next day. It doesn't matter; I don't work from nine to five. I have the freedom to do whatever I please. It's been said that money doesn't bring happiness. I disagree. Knowing that I can go wherever I want, get whatever I want, do whatever I want, makes me very happy indeed.

I take my time. I spend a long time in the shower and then dress in a pair of distressed Amiri jeans and a matching Burberry T-shirt. I plan to visit the gym later; keeping in shape is essential in my line of work. But before then, I contemplate breakfast.

I decide to visit my favourite restaurant and am pulling on my Ralph Lauren tailored jacket when there is a knock on the front door.

I freeze.

I'm not expecting anyone. I never have visitors; I make sure of that. It could be a delivery, but I've not ordered anything. I feel a twitch between my shoulder blades. Something isn't right. I can't explain it, I just know it. I've been in this game long enough to trust my instincts, so I immediately use the familiar finger gesture on my right hand and make a jump to another of my homes.

As soon as I make the jump, a sense of unease washes over me. The lounge of my second home materialises around me in less than a second, but the unease remains. There's something else. A presence that I can't quite pinpoint, like a shadow lurking just out of sight. I feel as though someone watched me make the jump, but there's no one here. The hairs on the back of my neck prickle. In all the jumps I've made in the past, I've never felt anything like this, and it tells me one thing: whoever knocked on my front door isn't an ordinary person.

For the first time in years, I don't feel safe. Even so, I've prepared for just such an occasion. I have many other places I can jump to. Places where no one knows me and where no one will ever find me.

I jump again to one of the most remote places I have at my disposal, a small, abandoned house on Foula, one of the Shetland Islands. No one knows me there, I've never visited. I bought it under a false name three years ago. There is absolutely nothing to connect me to this location.

I'm standing in the kitchen, or what was the kitchen. The place is practically a derelict. With no one to maintain it, over the years, it's gradually decayed. The room is covered in dust, rodent droppings, and cobwebs. Paint and wallpaper are peeling from the walls. There must be a problem with the roof, because there's evidence of water damage; the ceiling is bowed and cracked and one wall is black and mouldy where water has run down onto the floor, lifting some of the quarry tiles.

It's a wreck and I don't intend to stay here. I raise my right hand, watching the sunlight streaming through a broken window glinting from the rings. But before I can make the jump gesture with my fingers, I hear a knock on the kitchen door.

I stand, stock still.

I'm shocked. I can't believe it. There's only thirty-eight people on the island, well that's how many there were when I bought this place. The odds of one of those thirty-eight knocking on my door right now, at this moment, are infinitesimal. No. It's not an islander. It's someone else. Someone followed me when I jumped here.

There's no way I'm opening that door.

I visualise another location and complete the finger gesture.

It's dark, as I expected. I'm on the other side of the world in Australia. I take a step to the right, reaching out to trace my hand across the wall to find the light switch. The sudden brightness causes me to squint for a few seconds, revealing a well-appointed bedroom with a king-sized bed, ensuite and a walk-in dressing room.

I stand still for a few seconds, listening. All is quiet. After a full minute, I breathe a sigh of relief. I've escaped.

Walking down the stairs, I enter the kitchen and pull out my favourite whisky from a cupboard to pour myself a drink. I consider my options. While I may have escaped, it was clear I was being hunted, and by no ordinary person. Or was I? Could it all have been coincidence? The knocks on the doors could have been innocent. Perhaps a salesperson or a neighbour?

No. There were no neighbours in Foula. That knock on the door had to be someone after me.

Taking a sip of my drink and savouring the flavour and the warm sensation as the liquid travels down to my stomach, I consider what to do next. I could jump again, but running isn't the answer. I can't run forever. I'll run out of places to hide. What to do?

My blood runs cold when a knock at the door breaks the silence, interrupting my thoughts.

This time it's different. I need to find out who it is and figure out what to do about them. A concealed draw holds a Glock G43X semi-auto, a Sig Sauer P365 Macro, and several magazines. I snatch up the Glock and slap a magazine into the grip. Making sure that the safety is on, I slip it into the pocket of my Ralph Lauren jacket.

The knock sounds again.

I turn towards the door and draw in a deep breath. Placing my hand in my pocket, I grip the Glock in readiness. Then I step to the side of the door, unlock it and open it just two inches.

I'm surprised at what I see when I peer through the gap.

A striking tall man stands at the door, his caramel-coloured skin perfectly complementing his jet-black short beard and steel-grey eyes. However, it's not just his handsome appearance that draws my attention - he's dressed in a tuxedo with a crisp white shirt, black bow tie, and sharp black jacket and trousers.

I'd expected to see someone in body armour, or a uniform, but not this. This was completely unexpected and very at odds with the situation. It didn't make sense. If someone was chasing me, why would they do it dressed in a tuxedo?

The man smiles, exposing white, even teeth.

"Good evening, Adam," he says in a baritone voice.

He knows my name.

Once again, the hairs on the back of my neck rise. My first instinct is to flee once again.

"Please don't teleport again," he tells me as he looks at his watch. "I have a date."

It's not just his appearance that has taken me by surprise, it's also what he's saying. He has a date? What's he talking about? Why has he been following me? He's making it sound as though I'm an inconvenience. He can't be the police or a federal agency. So, what was going on?

"May I come in?" he asks, his eyebrows raised expectantly.

I hesitate. Despite his seemingly harmless appearance, he's probably equipped with advanced technology that allows him to not only jump but also track me. That makes him very dangerous and skilled. He could be concealing a weapon and who knows what else. Could I even stop him from coming in if I wanted to? He probably didn't need to knock. I let my gaze roam over his figure once more. He's clearly in good shape, and I'm sure there are powerful muscles underneath that perfectly fitted jacket and shirt.

I step aside and back up into the kitchen, careful to keep a reasonable distance between us, my hand still in my pocket holding onto the Glock. He enters nonchalantly, closing the door behind him.

"Can I have one of those?" he asks, pointing to the drink I've placed down on the countertop.

"Sure, help yourself," I nod.

He opens the drinks cupboard above the countertop and pulls out the whisky bottle. He didn't ask which cupboard contained the drinks; he already knew. Ice travels down my spine and my spider sense clamours in my brain - run!

He's so casual, his movements easy and confident as he pours his drink, raises it to his lips and sips at it, eying me over the top of the glass. Everything about him exudes self-assurance and control, as though he's used to situations like this. But I'm not! I've never encountered anyone like him before. I can't decide what to do. I could simply pull out the Glock and shoot him in the head, and for a few seconds I'm very tempted. But if I did that, I wouldn't find out what this was all about. Was he alone or was he employed by someone? If I killed him, would someone replace him? I have to find out.

"You aren't going to finish yours?" he asks.

I shake my head.

"Maybe you should tell me why you are here?" I ask, trying to sound calm.

He smiles.

"Straight to the point," he observes. "Very good. I am in a hurry." He gestures with his glass, the contents sloshing almost over the rim. "Should we move into the lounge, where we can be more comfortable?"

Something caught my eye when he gestured with his drink - the golden rings on his fingers. They're just like mine. But when his sleeves shifted, I glimpsed something else. A bracelet that's connected to the rings with delicate gold chains.

I was right. He has advanced tech. He has something better than my rings, or at least something similar but with more functionality. I bet that's how he tracked me and in hindsight I realise I did the right thing by letting him into my home. It would have been futile trying to escape someone who has access to such technology.

With my hand still in my pocket, I back slowly towards the lounge door. Stretching my arm behind me, I grasp the handle and carefully open the door, never once taking my eyes from the stranger standing in front of me. He watches and waits as I back through the door into the large lounge. I quickly flick on the lights and stride away from the door to position myself at the far end of the room. I'm not about to let him get too close.

It's a full ten seconds before he follows. Standing in the doorway, he surveys the room, then makes for the nearest easy chair and sits. He observes me as he takes another sip of his drink.

"Your caution is commendable, but unnecessary," his baritone voice rumbles. "But I'm not here to kill you. That much should be obvious."

A tiny part of me relaxes a little, but only a tiny part. This stranger is clearly dangerous.

"So, why are you here?" I ask.

He puts down his drink on a small table next to his chair and steeples his fingers.

"I'm here to make you an offer," he replies.

It's not the answer I expected.

"What kind of offer?" I ask warily.

"Let me begin by telling you my name," he answers, picking up his drink again. "I'm Adam, Adam Garcia."

It's another surprise. He can't be Adam Garcia, he just can't.

"Bullshit!" I exclaim.

He slowly nods and then drains his glass. I study him carefully. I suppose that there are a few similarities. The shape of his nose, maybe the way his black hair falls across his eyes occasionally, only to be removed by a quick shake of the head. But surely not? It must be a coincidence that he has the same name as me.

"That's right." He places the glass down with a clunk. "I can see that you see it now." He looks at his watch and frowns. "I've somewhere to be and I'm late already." He looks back up at me and steeples his fingers once more. "In the interests of time, let me explain." He pauses as if waiting for me to answer, then continues. "You and I are the same person. The only difference being the fact that you're a self-taught assassin and I'm world jumper and a narcissist."

He paused again. When I don't answer, he carries on.

"Have you heard of the multiverse?"

I nod.

"Well, I'm from one of those multiverses. I've jumped from my world to find you, another version of myself."

By now, I've had enough.

"That's just so much bullshit! The multiverse is a theory that's been around for years, but that's all it is, a theory!"

He flashes me a sad smile.

"Not theory, fact," he answers. "I'm living proof."

"Sure, you look a bit like me, but you have different skin colouring and we're not the same build," I scoff.

"Ah, that's because the world I'm from is a long way from this one. You and I diverged into separate worlds when we were five. The difference is thirty years of us living different lives. You became an assassin and I." He paused and grimaced slightly. "Let's just say that I turned out different."

I can tell that he's serious and means what he's saying, but I don't believe him. It's a total fantasy, it can't be true. That someone could travel between alternate worlds in the multiverse was preposterous. But then why is he here? He didn't chase me all over the world to spout nonsense at me. So why?

"I don't believe you," I tell him.

"Of course you don't." He stretches out his legs in front of him and folds his arms across his chest. "I could demonstrate, but before I do, I'd appreciate it if you would remove your hand from that weapon in your pocket." He smiles. "We wouldn't want you shooting me by accident, would we?"

I suppose I should have known that he would notice the Colt, but I'm not about to give it up. I don't trust this guy at all. He's given me no reason to believe that he won't suddenly jump up and try to kill me. I still don't know why he's here and what he wants. So, I pull a chair from the nearby dining table and sit, placing the colt on the table beside me. I rest my hand on the table, ready to snatch it up if needed.

"You'll forgive me if I keep it nearby?" I ask dryly. "After all, I still don't know why you're here."

He nods his acceptance.

"Of course. Perfectly understandable. I'd do the same if I were you. Oh wait. I am you!" He chuckles at his own joke, but I don't join in. Once more, I contemplate simply shooting him in the head. It would certainly resolve the current situation. But I also can't help but wonder if he's part of a group and that if I kill him, there would be others. No, I can't kill him. Not yet. I need to learn more first. But after I find out what's going on, I definitely intend to kill him.

"You've noticed my Assist?" he asks raising his eyebrows.

"Your what?"

He grins and rolls up his jacket and shirt sleeves on his right arm, revealing the bracelet that links to his rings - one on each finger. He wiggles his fingers and I feel a surge of fear. A memory resurfaces from when I purchased my own rings, and what the woman told me:

"With practice, you'll be able to teleport yourself anywhere, even across great distances. And it's also possible to use them for offence or defence."

At the time, I didn't believe her about the weapon capabilities of the rings. I've never tried it. I only wanted them for their teleporting ability. But maybe he has? Could he kill me with just a tiny gesture of his little finger? I move my hand closer to the Colt just in case.

"Don't panic, I've already told you I'm not here to kill you." His eyes flick to my hand, edging towards the Colt. "Try to contain yourself and not do anything stupid. I'm going to show you how I travel between worlds in the multiverse."

He pauses. I'm a little reassured that he's said he's not here to kill me again, but I don't relax.

He flicks his wrist and I'm startled to see a jet-black disc materialise hanging in the air in the middle of the room.

"This is a portal," he explains. "On the other side of it is another world. With my Assist, I can open portals between any world and travel through them. I travelled here, to your world, to find you."

For a while, I'm speechless. I gaze at the black disc, trying to process what I'm seeing. It seems as though he's telling the truth, but I'm not yet convinced. I lean back in my chair and pick up an empty vase from a small set of drawers nearby. He watches calmly as I heft it in my hand and then launch it at the black disc.

It disappears as it impacts the disc, clearly going straight through it.

Grudgingly, I'm beginning to think that he's telling the truth, or at least parts of what he's says is true. That disc is really something. The vase went through it, but where it ended up is anyone's guess.

He flicks his wrist and the disc fades to nothing, then glances at his watch again.

"That's enough. I'm sure that if you apply that brain of yours, you'll understand that I'm telling the truth and the implications of what I'm saying. Let's get down to business. It's getting late."

He pauses and eyes me over steepled fingers.

"Being the nasty, self-absorbed person I am, I can't abide the thought of other versions of me being around, even if they're all in different worlds. So, here's the offer."

He pauses once again, as if waiting for me to respond. When I don't, he continues.

"I want you to travel to travel to different universes and kill every other version of me."

My jaw drops in utter shock, my mouth hangs open. His words hit me like a ton of bricks, leaving me speechless. My mind races with confusion, thoughts swirling and colliding as I struggle to process what he just said. Everything is a blur, a jumbled mess of emotions and questions. He can't mean what he just said, can he? He wants me to kill versions of myself. That is, if I accept that he's a version of me.

I manage to marshal my thoughts somewhat to study him carefully. I try to ignore the obvious and instead concentrate on his mannerisms, the way he sits, his expression. Is that me? Do I stroke my chin like that? Do I cross my legs and move my foot in the same way as he does? After a few seconds, it slowly dawns on me that everything he's told me is true. The evidence is undeniable. He is me and I am him.

So, what am I to make of his offer?

The thought of killing doesn't faze me in the slightest. But versions of myself? That's a different story. It wouldn't be easy. I like to think of myself as both clever and careful. Tracking down versions of me would be hard enough, but then finding the right place and method for a kill would be harder still.

"Why me?" I ask him. "Why are you asking me to do this? And why would I do what you ask?"

He checks his watch again.

"Why indeed," he nods at me. "Let me ask you a question in order to answer yours. Are you bored?"

"Bored?"

He gives me a thin smile.

"With the lack of challenge. Aren't you finding it all too easy? There's no one in this world better than you. No one who can do what you can. You're un-catchable and unstoppable. You've amassed a huge amount of money, and you don't need anymore. What you lack, what you need, is something to challenge you, something to make your heart race and your mind think. Hunting and killing versions of yourself will be the ultimate challenge. It will be difficult and will require you to use every ounce of skill and cunning. Doesn't that sound like fun to you?"

That's quite a speech and I can't deny that some of his points hit home. He's right, I haven't felt challenged for a while. But did that mean I wanted to accept his offer?

"You have a point," I replied. "But I'm not convinced I want that level of challenge. What if I say no?"

His face grows serious.

"That is up to you, of course. If you say no, then I'll find another version of us who'll say yes. But." He fixes me with a stare. "I think we both know that you'll say yes."

I consider his words. He's so sure of himself, so confident. Almost as though he knows exactly how this little scene will play out, as though he's done this before. Something clicks in my mind.

"You've done this before!" I exclaim. "How many others have you approached?"

He grins.

"A few."

My eyebrows travel up to my hairline, and I gasp.

He nods, his grin fading, his eyes not leaving mine. I make another connection.

"You killed them?"

He tips his head to one side.

"Like I said, I can't abide the thought of other versions of me being around."

I digest this slowly, thinking about his words. He said them in a matter-of-fact manner, as though killing other versions of himself was a daily occurrence. But then, I kill as a profession and don't have any second thoughts for my victims. You could say that I'm callous, unsympathetic, or even a narcissist. Maybe that's not surprising, because we are the same person after all.

"What's your answer?" he asks. "Will you accept my offer? As if I didn't already know."

He's so sure of himself. I stare at him as he checks his watch yet again. But of course, he's right. I've already decided. I can't refuse his offer. It would be the ultimate test. I would hunt the hunter himself. There could be no greater challenge. He was right, my life was boring. Eventually, I'd become careless by taking greater and greater risks. Eventually, I'd either get caught or killed.

"Alright," I answer. "I'll do it."

He startles me by standing quickly. I automatically grab the Colt's grip.

"Excellent!" he exclaims in his deep voice. "I'll send you an upgraded Assist that will enable you to travel between worlds, meanwhile I have somewhere to be."

He flicks his wrist as before and another black disc appears. He strides towards it. Curiosity peaked. I can't help myself.

"Who's your date with?"

He laughs as he starts to step through the portal.

"I have a hot date with my boyfriend and I'm already late," he answers. He stops halfway through the portal and turns to me.

"You'll have your upgraded Assist tomorrow morning. I suggest you get started on your new mission straight away, because the others will be after you."

He steps through.

"What others?" I needlessly shout after him. The portal fades to nothing and I'm left alone with his words echoing in my mind. He's clever, far more than I gave him credit for. He's probably made this offer a hundred times before, maybe a thousand. Across the multiverse there are versions of me, all assassins, all on a mission to kill each other.

And all the while, he would be watching it all, enjoying the show. He gets to sit back and watch the chaos until he's the only one left.

Therapy

Week One

The young woman stepped into the opulent room, not noticing the rich decor and expensive furnishings. Every detail in the room exuded wealth and immaculate taste, from the intricately patterned silk wallpaper to the plush carpeting. Expensive artwork adorned the walls, most of which depicted animal scenes. In one, a herd of zebras galloped across a vast plain of dry, brown grass. In another, a pod of dolphins leapt and cavorted in the wash created by a prow of a ship. Yet another showed a mob of meerkats, all standing upright, their pointy noses looking directly at the viewer.

At one end of the spacious room sat a petite woman behind a large oak desk, her presence radiating confidence. In front of the desk were two comfortable-looking armchairs, and off to one side stood a chaise longue.

After entering the room, the young woman, shoulders slumped, head down, shuffled forward and practically fell into one of the two arms chairs. She sat, staring down at her hands clasped tightly before her in her lap. Her jeans had fashionable rips at both knees, and she wore a dirty, grey cardigan over a red t-shirt that seemed old and well worn, with sleeves that were a little too long.

The woman behind the desk appraised her patient carefully as she entered, noticing the shuffling gait, the rumpled clothes, matted hair, and chewed nails. Inwardly, she sighed. Here was another young person who desperately needed her help. The number of patients being referred to her had been growing steadily over the last few months, so much so that she was struggling to cope and had to cut down each consultation to just ten minutes each. It wasn't enough, she knew, but she was stuck between a rock and a hard place. With an ever-increasing caseload and no additional staff to help, there was no other choice. She would do her very best for every single patient that came into her office.

She rose from her chair, grabbing a notepad from her desk. Impeccably dressed in a tailored blue business suit and white blouse, she walked to the front of her desk and carefully positioned the second armchair so that it directly faced her patient. She sat down gracefully and crossed her legs.

"My name is Dr Beverley Chambers." She paused and read something from her pad. "I understand Dr Myers referred you to see me?"

When there was no answer, she continued.

"You are Deborah Foster? Dr Myers has informed me you've not been feeling yourself lately?"

She waited until it was obvious that there would be no answer, then she leaned forward and placed a hand gently on Deborah's arm.

"Deborah? Can you hear me?"

A breathy whisper that was barely audible.

"Debbie." The final syllable drawn out into a hiss so that her name sounded like "Debbeeee."

"It's nice to meet you, Debbie," replied Bev. "You can call me Bev. Would you like a drink? Maybe a tea or water?"

Debbie moved her head in a tiny movement from one side to another.

Bev sat back in her chair and considered her next words. It was already clear that this case was extreme.

"Okay, Debbie. Do you think you could answer some questions?"

Debbie mumbled a quiet response that was almost impossible to discern, but Bev thought she heard: "Whatever."

Bev opened her pad and took up her pen to scribble some notes. She looked up at her patient.

"What's been happening recently?" she asked. "I understand you passed your driving test two weeks ago?"

There was no reply from Debbie, who remained hunched over her hands in her lap, her long, greasy hair cascading around her face.

Bev frowned slightly.

"Debbie, do you know why you're here?"

There was an imperceptible nod.

"Good," she said, pursing her ruby red lips as she considered the situation once again. Clearly, this was a case that deserved more of her attention, one that might be career defining. It might even be something she could publish. But first, she would concentrate on reaching this young woman, help her overcome her trauma and help her assimilate back into society.

"I want you to know that I'm here to help you, but I can't do that if you don't answer my questions." She scribbled some notes on her pad, then set it down on her lap, inserting the end of her pen into her mouth to chew on it with perfect white teeth.

"Dr Myers has informed me about your recent traumatic event. He's assured me he and his team have done all they can for your physical injuries." Bev chewed at the pen as she talked, the action distorting her voice slightly. "If you'd give me a chance, I'd like to help you restore your mental wellbeing." She removed her pen from her mouth and stared intently at Debbie. "Would that be okay with you, Debbie?"

There was another imperceptible nod.

"Good. I won't be so crass as to ask you to recount your experience. But what I would like to ask you to do is to consider where you are right now." Bev paused, uncrossed her legs and recrossed them. "You're in a safe place. You can say anything or ask anything here. I won't judge you."

There was no acknowledgement from Debbie.

Bev considered her options. It was obvious that Debbie was badly affected by the trauma she'd endured, so much so that she could barely function.

"Debbie, do you have a safe place to stay?"

Another nod.

"Good."

Unfortunately, she was nearly out of time. Her next patient would be waiting in the anteroom. Forced by circumstances, she did the only thing she could. She stood and walked over to her desk. Placing her pad down, she pulled open a draw and extracted a prescription pad.

"I'm going to prescribe a strong anti-depressant. I want you to get them dispensed and start taking them straight away." She scribbled on the pad and then looked up at Debbie. "Will you do that for me, Debbie?"

Yet another nod.

Bev signed the script and held it out.

"You should be feeling better when we next meet in a week's time. I want you to be prepared for a more interactive session. I can't help you if you don't communicate with me."

She laid a hand lightly on Debbie's shoulder and squeezed gently.

"I really am here to help you. I've put my number on the bottom of your prescription. If your feelings become too much to cope with, I want you to call me. Any time of the day or night. Okay?"

Debbie's small hand snatched the paper from Bev, quickly secreting it inside a sleeve of her over large cardigan.

Week Two

Dr Beverley Chambers noticed the difference in Debbie as soon as she entered her office one week later. Her ripped jeans had been replaced with a long flowing gypsy skirt, her pink, over large cardigan now a tailored jacket made from jeans material.

While her long, black hair was still matted and tangled, she did, at least, hold her head up and make eye contact as she made her way to sit in the comfortable chair in front of the desk.

Bev smiled, leaned back in her expensive leather office chair.

"Hello, Debbie. It's so nice to see you again. How are you feeling?"

Debbie's eyes flicked to the floor.

"Better," she answered.

"Good, very good."

Bev rose from her seat and travelled around her imposing desk to join Debbie in the second chair. It surprised her that the medication had such a dramatic effect. Still, it was a win and she would take it. After all, drugs affected different people differently and the one that she had prescribed was powerful.

"Do you think you are up to answering a few questions?"

Debbie nodded, her eyes darting around the room, finally fixating on the painting of the Meerkats.

"I'd like to know more about the traumatic event you experienced. Do you feel you can share some details with me?"

"No!" Debbie cried out, her voice filled with fear, panic etched on her face, her eyes wide and her breath coming in quick gasps. Whatever had happened to her was still too fresh and too painful to discuss.

Bev quickly leaned forward and placed a hand on Debbie's arm. She had moved too quickly, pressed for time. She had tried to force the issue to get Debbie to talk. It was too soon. She back peddled quickly.

"It's okay Debbie. You don't have to if you don't want to. I meant what I said last time you were here. This is a safe place. You don't have to talk about anything that makes you uncomfortable."

Debbie appeared to relax a little. She wiped the back of a hand across her face, cleaning away the tears.

Bev leaned back in her chair, breathing a sigh of relief.

"Let's try something else. Are you having trouble sleeping or eating?"

"Sometimes," Debbie whispered a reply.

Bev wrote something on her notepad.

"What about thoughts of suicide? Do you think about taking your own life?"

Debbie nodded. She fixed her gaze once more upon the painting of the meerkats.

"Do you have a support system in place? What I mean is, do you have someone to talk to about your thoughts?"

Debbie slowly shook her head.

"No, not really."

"Your family, close friends, work colleagues?"

"I don't work," Debbie replied in a quiet voice, all the while not removing her gaze from the meerkats. "I'm an only child and my parents died five years ago in a car accident. I have no friends."

Bev scribbled on her pad some more and chewed on her pen.

"Do you think you would be open to exploring some treatment options? I mean, above the medication I prescribed?"

"Yes."

"Good. That's very good."

Bev put down her pad onto her knee.

"It might not seem like it right now, but you are making progress. I think that with the right treatment; a combination of medication and cognitive behaviour therapy, we will soon have you back on your feet." She paused, gazing intently at her patient. "I'm going to put you in contact with a support group. They meet on the weekends. It's full of people just like you. I think it will help you realise you aren't on your own. You'll be able to see that there are others who are going through the same issues as you."

She held up her hand when Debbie turned to her, tearing her gaze from the meerkats.

"Don't worry, you won't have to join in. You don't have to talk about anything until you are ready. I'd like you to go, anyway. Do you think you could do that?"

Debbie looked away and nodded slowly.

"Good," continued Bev. She checked her watch and frowned. "Please continue with the medication and I'll see you next week. Okay?"

Week Three

Dr Beverley Chambers couldn't hide the look of surprise on her face when Debbie walked into the room with a bounce in her step and a smile on her face.

Wearing a fashionable, tailored pink jacket over a white t-shirt, flared jeans and white trainers, she flopped into the chair with a contented sigh. Her bright, sparkling blue eyes flicked around the room before she gazed with confidence at Bev.

"Morning, Dr Bev," she said with a bright smile.

Bev was taken aback. The change was more than dramatic; it was hard to believe. Medication and group therapy rarely work this quickly. Something had changed. Debbie was like a different woman. The change was so striking.

"Good morning, Debbie," she replied. "You're obviously feeling much better?"

"Oh yes," answered Debbie enthusiastically. "Thanks to you."

"How so?" asked Bev.

"I've met someone."

Bev's eyebrows rose.

"Someone special?" she asked, taking up her pad and writing some notes.

Debbie nodded.

"I met her at the therapy session you sent me to. At first, I didn't like her. She can come across as a bit arrogant and superior, but once you get to know her, she's really nice."

Bev frowned.

"Is she a patient?"

"Oh yes. She told me she's been going to the group sessions for weeks. She had a breakdown six months ago."

Bev's frown deepened. She put the pen to her mouth and chewed the end. This was not at all what she expected, and she didn't like what she was hearing. She cleared her throat.

"I'm not sure that forming a relationship with another patient is a good idea. Particularly as they've been in therapy for so long."

Debbie nodded.

"Molly said you would say that. But you don't need to worry. I'm feeling much better. Molly's good for me."

Bev was becoming more and more worried. This didn't sound like a healthy relationship at all, and, in fact, it sounded as though Debbie was being manipulated by her new friend. This was something that she hadn't expected and, in her opinion, was a step backwards. Debbie obviously felt a lot better, but what would happen when Molly abandoned her as she inevitably would? Or worse? Debbie was in a vulnerable state. What were Molly's intentions? She made a note of Molly's name on her pad and determined to find out more about her after this session. For now, she wouldn't pursue the matter.

"How are you getting on with your medication? I would like to discuss reducing the dose if that's alright with you. I started you on a higher dose than I would normally prescribe."

Debbie flashed her a toothy grin.

"I gave up taking them three days ago."

Her answer startled Bev.

"What?" she exclaimed. "But why? I'm concerned that you're not ready to stop the medication I prescribed, let alone the issues that stopping suddenly can cause."

"Molly told me I don't need it anymore."

Bev fell silent. Things were a lot worse than she had initially thought. Molly was clearly manipulating Debbie already, and what she was doing was dangerous. She underlined Molly's name on her pad with three deep lines. She intended to find out who this Molly was and get her thrown off the programme. Who was the leader of that support group? She couldn't remember, but she also intended to talk to them too. There is no way they should have allowed this to happen. But all of that was in the future. What should she do now? What could she do? She knew that instructing Debbie to stop seeing Molly wouldn't work. Obviously, she was infatuated.

"Debbie, I want you to restart taking the medication I prescribed."

Debbie shook her head.

"Oh no, I'm not going to do that. Molly said I don't need it."

Bev fell silent once more. The situation was getting more and more serious. She would have to act, as the wellbeing of her patient was at stake.

"Very well, I'd like to refer you for some Cognitive Behavioural Behaviour treatment in place of the support group sessions you have been attending. I'm afraid you can't do both. What do you think?"

Bev expected Debbie to protest, to say something about her not being able to meet Molly. But instead, she instantly agreed.

"Okay, everything you've recommended so far has helped, so I'll give it a go."

"Good," replied Bev, relieved that she'd been able to make some progress. Straight after this consultation, she'd be doing everything she could to get rid of Molly. Her next appointment would have to be cancelled. She wrote the meeting details on a card and passed it to Debbie.

"I'll see you next week."

Week Four

As her office door swung open, Bev was shocked at Debbie's appearance. Instead of walking in, she lingered in the doorway, her slender form outlined by the faint light behind her. Despite the contrast, Bev could still make out her clothing, which comprised a bright red crop top exposing her midriff, and a short black skirt with an asymmetric hem that started at her left knee and ended at her right hip. Large, heavy-looking black boots completed the look.

When she eventually entered the room, she did so with a swagger. Her big boots clomping down as she strode to her usual chair, her hips swaying from side to side. Once sat, she crossed her legs and ran her hand over her completely shaven head, staring straight at Bev with heavily mascaraed eyes, almost daring her to say something about her new look.

Bev couldn't believe the total transformation before her. It wasn't just the clothes, even her features seemed to have changed, her skin appeared to be smoother and more toned. Every movement was deliberate and graceful, with a new sense of confidence and poise. Bev couldn't believe this was the same person who had graced her office just four weeks ago. The change was nothing short of breath-taking, a metamorphosis that left Bev speechless and mesmerised all at once.

Once she had got over the shock and could think clearly, Bev knew that something was wrong. Debbie should not be behaving as she should. Nothing she had prescribed, the medication or the therapies, should have had such a dramatic effect. No, what was happening here was something else, and that something could only be one thing. Molly. Bev's lips thinned as she recalled her meeting.

Molly was a tall and imposing young woman, beautiful, composed and someone who definitely did not need to attend group therapy sessions. Bev had immediately classified her in her mind as a predator. Someone who preyed on the vulnerable, probably for money or sex, but almost certainly for the thrill of the control.

The silence between them lengthened to a full three minutes before Bev could finally speak.

"Hello Debbie, I see that you've made one or two changes."

Debbie's stern expression changed, a self-satisfied grin spreading over her face.

"Do you like it?" she asked, playing with a set of gold rings adorning her right hand.

"Well, it's certainly different and very bold. I'm guessing that you are feeling much better. The Cognitive Behaviour Therapy is working?"

Debbie waved her hand in a dismissive gesture.

"I didn't go to those silly sessions. I'm fully healed. I came here today to say goodbye and to thank you for your help."

Bev's eyebrows raised.

"I really think that it's far too soon for you to stop treatment and I'm concerned that you didn't attend the CBT. Four weeks is not enough time for you to recover from your trauma."

Debbie sat back in her chair and grinned back at Bev.

"My trauma is gone, and my recovery is complete. I've reassigned the bad memories and made sure that it can't happen again."

Bev cursed herself inwardly. She had underestimated Molly, her warning had obviously been ignored, and she had continued to influence poor Debbie. And now Debbie was completely under her spell, probably believing everything she was told.

"Debbie, what do you mean when you say you've reassigned the bad memories?"

"I catalogued them and filed them away so that they don't bother me anymore. It's actually quite easy once you know how."

Bev's heart sank. This was far worse than she had thought. It was a complete disaster. At some point in the near future, Debbie would realise that she'd been lied to, that she'd been deceived, manipulated and used. By then, it would be too late. Her already fragile mind would shatter, and she would probably experience a psychotic episode from which she might not recover. Already she was talking nonsense, probably fed to her by Molly. Bev realised she had to find a way of reversing the damage already done, but how? She decided to tackle things head on.

"You can't just file away memories, as you suggested. I'm worried that you might think that you're recovered because someone has told you something that may not be true. And I'm worried that you could relapse at any time. I would like you to think carefully about what you are doing. It's very dangerous."

Debbie's laughter took Bev by surprise. She had expected her to be angry and insolent, for her to argue and maybe even storm out. Instead, she threw back her bald head and practically guffawed at the ceiling.

"What's so funny?" asked Bev. She was starting to feel annoyed. First Molly was interfering with her patient and now she was being laughed at.

Debbie stopped laughing suddenly and looked pointedly at Bev.

"I knew you were going to say that, just as I know that you're getting annoyed. You want me to stop seeing Molly? You think she's bad for me and influencing me in ways that could be dangerous for my health." She paused and tapped her booted foot, a thoughtful look on her face. "I suppose you couldn't know. You haven't got one of these." She held up her right hand, showing off her rings.

"A ring?" Bev asked, puzzled.

Debbie laughed again.

"No, silly, not just one ring, five. Molly gave it to me. She calls it an Assist."

Bev frowned. This was nonsense. Was Debbie already losing touch with reality? Was this the start of a psychotic break?

"Debbie, do you know what you're saying?"

Debbie nodded enthusiastically, smiling like a Cheshire cat.

"Of course. Dr Bev, you don't need to worry about me. I don't need any more treatment. You've helped me get better and I wouldn't have met Molly if not for you. Molly is special. I've finally met someone who's supportive and loves me for who I am. She showed me how to deal with that man."

Bev grew increasingly concerned as Debbie continued speaking. It was now very clear that Molly was the one pulling the strings, and Bev knew this would not end well. But it was Debbie's last statement that really alarmed her. What was she saying? Did she even know what she was saying?

"Please tell me you haven't done anything stupid. You know the police told you that you shouldn't approach your attacker, and it wouldn't help you recover. I certainly wouldn't recommend it." Bev paused and then continued. "You haven't, have you?"

Debbie shrugged.

"Let's just say that he won't be bothering anyone else and that I feel much, much better."

Bev stood suddenly, her hand going to her mouth, her eyes wide. Surely Debbie wasn't saying what she thought she was?

"What do you mean?" she asked in a squeaky voice.

Debbie smiled grimly; her eyes bright as she folded her arms over her chest. She fixed Bev with a piercing stare.

"I think you know what I mean," she answered. "Molly showed me how. No one's going to miss that low life."

"Oh, my god Debbie! This is awful. You can't mean that you killed him! I can't help you when you're in jail!"

Debbie rose from her chair, smoothing down her skirt.

"You don't understand Dr Bev. I won't be going to jail, and I'm fully recovered. I see now that it was a mistake coming to see you one last time."

"Wait!" Bev shouted. "Don't go. You've a completely mistaken understanding of your recovery. You could relapse, you need my help. I can't let you leave after confessing to murder! As a practicing psychiatrist, it is my responsibility to provide a duty of care. I must report you to the police!"

Debbie looked across the desk at Bev, a look of pity and amusement on her face.

"Oh dear. You seem to think that you can stop me?" With one-inch heeled boots, she was a good five inches taller than Bev. She struck an imposing figure, dressed as she was, her shiny bald head glinting from the overhead lights. She turned and walked to the door. When she reached it, she turned back to face Bev.

"You won't be seeing me again. I wouldn't advise calling the police. Molly wouldn't like it."

With a pointed finger, she gestured towards the phone sitting on the desk. There was a loud crack, causing Bev to flinch, and a puff of black smoke wafted up from the phone. Before she could say anything, Debbie continued.

"Your phone won't work. Goodbye Dr Bev."

As she turned to exit the room, Bev called out.

"What did you just do? You can't leave, you're not recovered!"

Debbie stopped in the doorway. Turning once more, she waved her right hand, the golden rings on her fingers flashing under the lights.

"You have no idea what I'm capable of now that I have this." She wriggled her fingers, tiny gold chains clinking against the rings. She tipped her head to one side.

"I think I'll go find out."

Life Before

Why did it always happen suddenly? Even on a day like this, with the sky a deep blue and the sunshine blazing. The coffee, hot and creamy, the Danish, warm and sweet, the chair, soft and comfortable. Even the chatter in the Costa coffee shop provided a soothing background of white noise, like the gentle crash of waves on a beach.

All of that meant nothing when, without warning, the wave of grief hit him like a pile driver. The tears came fast, streaming down his stubbled cheeks, plopping onto the wooden table before him. He brought up his shaking hands to cover his mouth and nose, trying and failing to muffle the gut-wrenching sobs that shook his entire body.

People at nearby tables glanced over with concern, but he kept his head down, trying to avoid any attention. He tried desperately to push the grief away to stifle the sobs and stop the tears, but it was useless. Just like all the other times, he was wasting his time. Just willing it to go away was impossible; he couldn't control it.

He had to get out.

He knew the pattern; it was always the same. It always hit without warning. Then there would be the tears and the crying. Soon after, there would be the anger. He would be so angry that he would see everything through a red mist. His blood would boil, his face red, sweat beading his forehead, his leg and arm muscles shaking with adrenalin. The rage burning through him like a fire in a straw house. It would consume him. He would become someone else. An uncontrollable animal bent on one thing: destruction and mayhem.

Finally, there would be the remorse. The overwhelming misery and regret causing him to descend into a black pit of depression that could last for days.

He had to get out before the rage started.

He jumped up from his seat, shaking the table, his cup and plate rattling loudly. His chair squeaked, the legs scraping on the floor as he pushed it back. He raced towards the exit. All eyes were on him as he crashed through the door. He didn't notice the pain from his elbow when he smashed it against the door frame.

There was no time to get back to his home. He knew that the rage wasn't far away. He could feel it building in his chest like a volcano about to erupt. Tears streaming down his cheeks, the sobs wracking his chest; he gave up all pretence that there was nothing wrong and ran full pelt to his car.

When he reached the Range Rover, he slammed into the driver's door, unable to stop in time, his anger almost taking over. It was fortunate that his car had keyless entry. Finding and then inserting a key into the lock was beyond him. He threw himself across the two front seats and just managed to shut the door behind him before the red mist descended and the fury hit him like a train.

When he came to his senses, the car was a mess. Shreds of paper, plastic, and strips of seat fabric littered both the passenger's and driver's footwells. The laptop bag he had stashed under the passenger seat was torn apart; its contents strewn across the seats. His laptop lay broken, with the screen detached from the base and bent almost in half, leaving shards of plastic and glass scattered everywhere. He grunted in pain as he struggled to sit up, noticing that his fingers were bleeding with broken nails. Some were missing, one barely hanging on by a thin piece of skin. The deep scratch marks on the dash and the rips in the seats clearly accounted for the state of his fingers.

He was hot and sweaty, the heat of the sun heating the air inside the car until it was almost unbearable. He pressed the button to roll down the window next to him and cooler air rushed in. The cool breeze felt refreshing against his skin, but when he wiped away the sweat from his face, he was surprised to see blood on his palm mixing with the blood from the ends of his fingers. In the rear-view mirror, he saw three long scratches down his right cheek, the blood pooling in his stubble.

He drew in a shaky breath. It had been a bad one and he could feel the sadness and depression descending upon him as was usual after the rage. Gingerly, mindful of his fingers and wincing at the pain, he fastened his seat belt and started the engine. His only thought was to get home. He ached all over and his fingers and face were throbbing. Exhausted, his head spiked with pain. He needed painkillers, a hot bath, and sleep.

Standing off to one side on the pavement, a woman with a shocked expression stared at him, her hand over her mouth. Behind her, a man was speaking on his mobile phone, gesticulating wildly towards the Range Rover. It was time to go. Placing the car in drive, he eased forward out of the parking space, ignoring the spectators. His antics had drawn a crowd. A group of teenagers were laughing and pointing. A homeless man shouted as he drove past.

"What's wrong with you, man?"

At his home, his priority was attending to his wounds. He cleansed them with an antiseptic solution and then relaxed in a hot bath for an hour, allowing the warm water to soothe his aching body. After drying off with a towel, he climbed into his luxurious king size bed, feeling comforted by the cool sheets that were lightly scented with lavender.

Before he closed his eyes, he gazed for a long moment at the photograph on the bedside table. It showed himself in a dark suit and tie, gazing adoringly at a stunning woman who was looking straight into the camera with sparkling blue eyes and a breathtaking smile. Her long blonde hair fell over her bare shoulders, giving her the appearance of a Viking queen. She wore a beautiful white wedding gown and held a bouquet of delicate white flowers. At the bottom of the photo were the words: Mark & Nicola.

One week later, he was sitting at a table in his local pub, drinking with his best friend.

"Look, Mark. You've gotta get over her. It's been eighteen months. I know it's hard, but you need to get back out there, have some fun."

Mark stared morosely into his pint glass, not really listening to his friend.

"There'll never be anyone like my Nicola, Dan," he replied.

Dan took a sip from his glass.

"Of course there is. There's lots of fish in the sea. You could at least take a swim."

Mark couldn't help grinning.

"You always had a way with words." He drew in a deep breath and lifted his pint glass. "Nic was the only one for me. I'm pretty sure that the other fish can't live up to her."

"But Mark, mate, you can't go on like this. Look at yourself." He gestured at Mark's face where the three scratches had healed to become three red lines. "You need to do something to take your mind off things. I know Nic meant everything to you and her death was tragic, but come on, man. This can't go on."

Mark took a long pull from his glass and set it down on the table.

"I know you're trying to help. But I can't move on. She was amazing. There was only one like her. She can't be replaced."

Dan lifted his beer and sat back in his seat, taking slow sips from the glass. He seemed deep in thought, as if pondering something, his brow furrowed. His eyes roved around the quiet interior of their local, then his eyes cut back to Mark. His lips pursed, and he leaned forward.

"What if I told you there might be a way to get her back?" he whispered conspiratorially.

Mark smiled wryly at his friend.

"Yeah right. This isn't something you can take the piss about."

Dan leaned further forward, his chest resting on the table.

"No, really." He gave the room another furtive glance. "I'm serious." He paused, then continued. "I wasn't going to say anything. It's pretty wild, but I know someone."

"For fuck's sake Dan!" Mark breathed. "Stop talking bollocks!"

"I'm not talking bollocks!" replied Dan urgently. "You remember that company I did the tax returns for last year? The one that was in trouble?"

Mark nodded.

"Sure. What were they called? Something silly like Life Ever After?"

"That's the one. Life Before."

"So what? What about them?"

"Well, obviously, I got a good look at their books. There were some very odd transactions. I had to interview some of their key people to get an understanding of what they were spending their money on."

Mark downed the last of his drink and placed his empty glass down on the table with a loud thunk.

"For fuck's sake, what are you talking about?"

Dan pulled his chair around so that he was sitting close to Mark.

"I found out something."

Mark looked quizzically at Dan.

"They can bring people back!" Dan whispered.

Mark was at a loss for words. What was his friend trying to say? Had he had one too many drinks? He leaned back, studying Dan's face with a sceptical eye, but all he saw was Dan staring earnestly at him, his eyes wide and glassy.

"Dan, I know you're trying to make me feel better, but this is going too far. You can stop now."

"Look," continued Dan. "I know how this sounds, and I wasn't sure that I should say anything about this. I don't want you to get your hopes up. But it's true. I actually spoke with the lead researcher. She was a bit odd and obviously didn't tell me they brought people back, but I'm not stupid. I worked it out. I even met someone who'd come back!"

"What? Back from death? That's impossible!"

"I don't know any of the technical details, so I don't know how it's done. But one time I was in their refectory eating a sandwich and I overheard two technicians talking."

"What about?"

"They were excited because they had just completed some sort of test. They were talking about travelling somewhere and bringing someone back with them."

"That means nothing!" Scoffed Mark. "They could have been talking about going to Australia!"

Dan nodded.

"Yes, they could. But the next day I bumped into someone in a corridor. I wasn't looking where I was going, and she was running. We crashed into each other, both falling to the floor. I helped her up, but she was acting strange. Her hair was wild, and she looked frightened. I asked if she was okay, she just looked at me and said: 'They shouldn't have brought me here, I was better off dead!' And then she ran off."

Mark thought about what Dan was trying to tell him. Was he saying what he thought he was?

"So, what are you saying?"

"I'm saying," Dan whispered urgently. "That I think you can get Nic back!"

Mark's fingers trembled as he took on board what Dan had said. Could it be possible? Could he get Nic back?

"Get the next round in. I need to think about this," He instructed Dan.

———

It took two months to set up a meeting.

Reaching out to Life Before directly was not an option. Dan informed him that their research was classified and highly confidential. No one was supposed to know what they were up to. They couldn't just walk in. For all Mark knew, it could be illegal. No. The only way to do this would be to contact someone on the inside, someone who could be susceptible to bribery or coercion. Fortunately, Dan knew just the person.

"You have no idea what you're getting into," said the man sitting in front of him.

Mark smiled grimly.

"Why don't you tell me?"

The man pushed his coffee mug to one side and leaned forward over their table, whispering urgently.

"Life Before is owned by an incredibly wealthy and powerful man. He setup the company four years ago and tasked us to do the impossible under the most difficult conditions I have ever worked in. Should he find out? Well, let's just say he has his own security detail. And that's not to mention that I'm bound by a strict confidentiality agreement. If I disclose any of our systems or technology, I'm finished!"

He looked around furtively.

"And you could have chosen a more private meeting place!"

Mark observed the man sitting before him in the coffee shop keenly. He was small, bald, with chubby cheeks and wore wire-rimmed glasses. He had a habit of holding his arms close to his sides, his hands in front of him. It had the unfortunate effect of making him look a little like a hamster. He had introduced himself as Professor Lucas, one of the lead scientists at Before Life.

"I'm not interested in the technology," replied Mark, noticing the look of surprise on the scientist's face.

"You aren't? Then what do you want?"

"I've heard that your," he paused, then continued. "Whatever it is, I understand that you've been successful, and you've brought someone back."

The professor looked alarmed.

"How do you know that?" he hissed angrily. "That's a closely guarded secret. No one knows, not even the technicians."

Mark smiled thinly.

"Let's just say I have my sources." He folded his arms on the table and leaned towards the scientist. "I want you to bring someone back for me."

Professor Lucas looked startled. Then he laughed a loud, almost manic laugh that caught the attention of people sitting at nearby tables. He quickly recovered.

"Impossible!" he wheezed through clenched teeth.

"Nothing's impossible, doc," said Mark.

"You don't know what you're asking," replied the professor angrily. "The security is too tight. It can't be done."

"In my experience, anyone can do anything if the price is right."

There was a moment of silence as the two men stared at each other across the table.

The professor finally spoke up, breaking the tense silence. "You can't afford it," he said, shaking his head. "I'd have to bribe several of my colleagues and then disappear entirely. The technicians would know it was me - everything is meticulously recorded. I'd have to leave the country and find a safe place to retire. It would mean the end of my career."

"Try me." Mark was unfazed.

The professor considered for a moment before replying.

"Ten million."

Mark didn't even blink.

"Your company owner is not the only wealthy person. If you deliver, then I agree. Ten million."

The professor felt shocked. He hadn't thought that the answer would be yes. If he accepted, he would have to think of a fool proof plan. One that would allow him to bypass the security staff and protocols, bring back whomever this person was, somehow get them out of the facility, hand them over. All without being caught. It would be no simple task. It was fraught with danger and risk, but ten million would allow him to escape to somewhere he would never be found. A place where he could rebuild his life.

"Alright, I'll do it. Who's the person you want me to bring back?"

Mark stood and held out his hand. He waited until the professor took it and shook it firmly. He grinned.

"Excellent. I want you to bring back my wife."

———

Six long months later, Mark sat in his Range Rover, waiting. The seat and dash had long since been repaired and were as good as new. Trying to keep his growing excitement under control, he checked his watch for the umpteenth time: ten past two in the morning. The professor was late.

They had planned to meet at this remote location at two in the morning, where he would finally be reunited with his wife, Nicola.

If all went according to plan, that is. He didn't ask for details; there was nothing he could do to help, anyway. He was completely reliant on the professor following through on the deal and carrying out his successful plan.

As the minutes ticked away, one by one, he couldn't shake off the feeling that something had gone wrong. He stared out of the car window at the trees illuminated by the moonlight and wondered if the professor had taken off with the money. Four months ago, he had transferred half of it. It was enough to make anyone reconsider their actions. The professor could have easily broken his promise and disappeared. Mark wouldn't be able to do anything about it. It's not as if he could go to the police.

When it was three am, Mark could feel the familiar rage build. By now, he was certain that the professor had run off with the money. He wasn't coming and he would never see Nicola again. It had all been a pipe dream. Dan should never have mentioned Life Before. He had allowed himself to believe that it was going to happen. He would never be with his wife again. It was a mistake to have been so trusting. He felt scammed. He bet that the professor, if he really was a professor, had he seen his qualifications? Did he even work at Life Before? He bet he was laughing right now. Probably sitting on a private jet, drinking champagne.

He slammed the steering wheel with his left hand and smashed his forehead against the door window as the anger hit him like a freight train. The safety glass of the window shattered into a multitude of tiny chunks that flew everywhere when he drove his right elbow straight through it.

Then a pair of headlights heading down the lane towards him brought him to his senses, his anger evaporating, to be replaced with a surge of elation and excitement. Yes! This must be the professor he had come through after all! He could barely contain his excitement opening the driver's door with trembling hands, chunks of glass tinkling onto the tarmac.

Mark shaded his eyes as the car approached, its bright headlights blinding him. He heard the driver's door open and shut before a shadowy figure emerged, backlit by the blinding lights. He was relieved when he recognised the figure as the professor.

"You made it! Do you have her?" He asked eagerly, peering intently into the headlights, unable to see if the passenger seat was occupied.

"Yes, yes!" replied the professor, irritated. "The money first! I was lucky to get out of there with my life. I've been shot! I had no idea the security guards carried guns!"

When he looked closer, Mark spied blood running down the side of the professor's face where a bullet had grazed his ear.

"Is Nicola okay?" he asked, full of concern and worry. "Why didn't she get out of the car with you?"

"She's fine. It's just a flesh wound. She'll live. Now transfer the money quickly. I need to get out of here."

Mark felt a surge of anger.

"She's wounded? You were supposed to bring her back, not get her killed!"

The professor waved an arm dismissively.

"She's alive. That's all that matters. Transfer the money and give me your car keys!"

"That's not part of our agreement. You were supposed to deliver my wife unharmed. That's the deal," growled Mark.

"The deal," the professor replied through gritted teeth. "Was for me to bring your wife back. I don't have time to discuss this anymore. You can't imagine what I had to go through to get her here." He pulled out a pistol from beneath his jacket. "Give me your keys and transfer the money." With his other hand, he threw a set of keys at Mark, who caught them automatically. "You can take my car. I can't afford to be followed."

For a moment Mark considered rushing him, but he realised that the distance was too great. There was no way he could avoid being shot. He'd been caught off guard. He hadn't considered that the professor would carry a gun. There was nothing he could do. Resignedly, he reached into his pocket and pulled out his phone. A few taps saw the remaining five million transferred.

"Okay, you have your money. What now?"

The professor checked his own phone, confirming that he had received the money.

"Throw over your keys. Your wife is in the backseat of my car. Go to her."

Mark hesitated. He guessed that the Life Before security personnel would be looking for the professor's car. If he took it, he might be caught. On the other hand, Nic was waiting for him, and the professor had the gun.

He removed his keys from his trouser pocket and threw them over, then made for the professor's car.

"Well played, Doc," he shouted over his shoulder. "Just know that if my wife isn't here or if you've hurt her, I will find you and I will kill you."

Mark's excitement grew rapidly as he approached the car. The professor was forgotten. His hand trembled as he reached for the rear door handle, and he found himself repeating a silent mantra of "please, please, please." She had to be here, she just had to be. When he wrenched open the rear door, relief and emotion flooded over him, and a sob escaped his lips. There she was, curled up and wrapped in a blanket, her long, thick blonde hair cascading over the seat.

His elation evaporated when he saw her eyes were closed, her face unnaturally pale. As he reached a trembling hand to the blanket and gently pulled it from her shoulders, he was shocked to see the blood.

Mark read the note again. By now, he had read it so many times he could practically recite it word for word, and he still found it hard to believe, yet alone understand.

If you are reading this, then I have been successful and have brought your wife back. There are, however, some things you should know. Technically, I haven't brought her back from the dead. That's not possible. But while your wife is dead in this world, she isn't dead in others.

Let me explain in terms your simple intellect can understand. We live in a multiverse which is an infinite series of universes or worlds that lie next to our own. Each world is different, based upon the choices we make or events that take place, with the world's closest to us being more similar to ours than the ones furthest away. Using the Life Before facilities, I located a world close to our own where your wife was still alive, but you were dead. I travelled to that world and brought her back with me.

Your wife knows everything. She knows that she's in a different world from her own and she knows you are alive in this one. You might notice some small differences in her behaviour and memories. After all, for her, you have been dead for two years. She might be quite different from your dead wife.

Based on my experience, your imagined reunion and future may not go as you expect.

This is your problem. Don't try to find me. I can't and won't help you. You will have to live with the consequences of your decisions.

Mark closed his eyes and tried to process for the hundredth time what the professor was trying to tell him. What did he mean by the words: *your imagined reunion and future may not go as you expect?* Shaking his head, he folded the note and tucked it into the pocket of his shirt, pushing all thoughts of it out of his mind. Nicola's return was all that mattered now.

He gazed over at the hospital bed from his seat. She was just as lovely as he remembered, with her long, blonde hair cascading over the pillow and her features relaxed as she slept. He couldn't wait for her to wake up. It shouldn't be long now. The bullet had missed her heart, but it had shattered a rib and lodged itself near her spine. The surgery had gone well, and the doctors had informed him she should make a full recovery.

It had taken some creative thinking to explain her injury and to get rid of the professor's car. He informed the police that they had been mugged. He couldn't tell them that Nicola was his wife - she was supposed to be dead, so he told them she was his girlfriend. They had been approached by a gang of youths who had taken his car and shot his girlfriend when she had refused to give up her phone. Later, he charged Dan with disposing of the professor's car by dumping it and torching it, making sure that there would be none of Nicola's DNA to be found.

He was in the clear. All the loose ends were tied off, and he had Nic back. It was perfect. In a few days, she would be well enough to go home, and they would resume their idyllic life. He smiled to himself and sighed contentedly. Everything was just as he had hoped it would be.

A whispered voice came from the bed.

"What are you smiling at?"

She was awake, her head turned to one side, her deep blue eyes staring at him, an impassive expression on her face. He broke into a wide smile and reached across to take her hand in his.

"Hello beautiful, how are you feeling?"

"Like shit!"

He grimaced sympathetically.

"I'm not surprised you've been shot. Professor Lucas should have taken better care of you."

Her expression didn't change.

"It wasn't his fault."

"I'm sure it was, my angel. If it weren't for him, you wouldn't be where you are now."

For a moment she didn't reply, just stared at him, her eyes cold and emotionless.

"If it weren't for him, I wouldn't be here now." She agreed.

"Concentrate on getting better. The sooner you're recovered, the sooner you can come home."

"I won't be coming home," her whispered voice was firm.

Mark frowned.

"What do you mean? Of course you're coming home."

There was a tiny shake of her head and a small, thin smile. She pulled her hand from his.

"I know what you've done."

His frown deepened.

"You mean I've brought you back?" he asked.

"You know what I'm talking about. You tried in my world. But guess what? You failed."

A chill passed through him, ice water trickling down his spine. A feeling of dread came over him. He released her hand and sat back in his chair. This can't be happening. His moment of bliss, of serenity, of happiness evaporated as he realised what she was saying. She knew. And now he understood what the professor had meant in his note: *your imagined reunion and future may not go as you expect.*

A soft buzzing noise sounded above the bed. She had pressed the call button.

"You're going to pay for what you did. I'm going to make sure of it."

He was speechless, his eyes widening as her face finally showed emotion. It wasn't love or happiness; it was pure hatred.

A petite brunette nurse burst into the room, making straight for her patient.

"You're awake. How are you feeling? Do you need anything?" She busied herself checking a drip and other monitoring machines.

Nicola turned towards her.

"Could you ask this man to leave? I don't want him here."

"I thought he was your boyfriend?" asked the nurse, a deep frown on her face.

"No," replied Nicola coldly. "I'm sure that's what he told you, but it's not true, not anymore. We broke up four months ago. He's been stalking me ever since."

The nurse glared at Mark.

"Sir?" asked the nurse sternly. "Respectfully, I'd like you to leave." She tipped her head sideways. "Please don't make me call security."

Mark was in disbelief. He couldn't believe what Nicola was saying. It was clear that she meant every word she had said. She was going to make his life hell. He saw his hopes for a future shatter. He realised now that it had been a mistake to bring her back, but there was no going back now. Determination set in as he knew he needed to fix things, just as he had done once before.

His face flushed with anger and his hands shook as he stood. Glaring at the nurse, his lips pressed tightly together, and his fists clenched, he strode to the door and pulled it open.

"I'll be seeing you," he growled, his tone ominous and deep.

Once the door closed behind him, the nurse turned to her patient.

"Do you want me to call the police?" she asked.

Nicola gave a tired smile.

"No, it's okay, but I don't want you to let him in again."

"Consider it done. I hate men like that. Was it a rough breakup?" The nurse picked up a jug of water from the bedside table and poured some into a plastic cup. "Would you like some water?"

Nicola nodded.

"I told him I didn't love him anymore and that I'd met someone else. You can imagine his reaction."

"Uh huh, I surely can."

She held Nicola's head up slightly, allowing her to sip the water through a straw. Nicola swallowed gratefully, licking her lips.

The nurse set the cup aside and extracted a pen from her breast pocket while walking to the foot of the bed.

Nicola smiled inwardly. It was all going to plan.

When the professor had visited her in her world, she had been awed and elated to learn about the multiverse. With the police closing in, slowly piecing the evidence together, it was just a matter of time before they drew the inevitable conclusion that she had murdered her husband. The professor offered a way out, a way to escape being caught and spending the rest of her life behind bars. So, she had eagerly agreed.

That Mark was alive in this world was a bonus. Here was another chance to put things right. Another chance to remove that bastard. It would be too late to save her duplicate in this world. The professor had explained that she was dead. That didn't surprise her. She knew about Mark's anger, had experienced it first-hand. She knew with certainty that he had killed her because that was exactly what he had tried to do to her.

She recalled the horror of that night. The way he had transformed into a wild animal full of hate and venom. The wild eyes, the frothing mouth and bared teeth. His fists flailing wildly, the fingers clawing at her face.

She didn't regret thrusting the kitchen knife into his chest. He deserved it.

Yes, she had made the right choice in coming to this new world. Here, she was free from suspicion. She had escaped and could start a new life. There was only one thing in her way - The Mark that lived in this world.

But not for long. She would see to that.

Afterward

I hope you have enjoyed reading this collection of stories as much as I enjoyed writing them. If possible, please consider leaving a review on Amazon. Reviews greatly assist me in selling more books.

Thank you for taking the time to read my work.

Stay in touch with the latest news by joining my Facebook group: Search for "psi war", select Sci-Fi Novels (Psi War).

Visit: http://www.twauthor.com
Email me at: psiwarbook@gmail.com

Other novels and short stories that are available now:

Awakening: Psi War Book 1
Worlds: Psi War Book 2
The Cara Files: File 1 - The Chase
The Cara Files: File 2 - Automata
The Cara Files: File 3 - Starship
The Bekkatron
The Ghost Hunter

Coming soon:

Together: Psi War Book 3
The Cara Files: File 4 – Lost

Printed in Great Britain
by Amazon